'Sorry, I didn't have time to make the bed,' he apologised gruffly.

Nikki bit her lip, staring at the thrown-back covers, the mind-blowing thought striking her that she wouldn't have minded climbing into Liam's bed just the way it was. And where on earth did she think she was going with *that* scenario?

Unfolding her clenched hands, she held her palms against the tops of her thighs. 'Thanks—I'm sure I'll find everything.'

A beat of silence.

'Hell…' Liam pressed his fingertips against his eyes and then scrubbed them over his cheekbones. 'This feels about as unnatural as trying to knit with toothpicks.'

'What does…?' Her heart kicked and she swallowed.

'You and me,' he said, his eyes tangling with hers, 'standing here discussing sleeping arrangements as though we were never more than *just friends*.' He gave a bleak smile. 'Does the wanting ever stop, Nik?'

DOCTORS DOWN UNDER

In Medical Romance™ you'll find a special kind of
doctor. Flying doctors, bush doctors, family doctors
and city specialists from Sydney, Brisbane and
Auckland. Whether they're battling with life
and love decisions in the hot and harsh locations
of the wilderness, or dealing with the personal
and medical dramas of city life, they exude a
determination, dedication and an earthy charm
that only comes from Down Under.

DOCTORS DOWN UNDER—

They're irresistible

From Mills & Boon® Medical Romance™

CHRISTMAS IN THE OUTBACK

BY
LEAH MARTYN

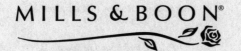

MILLS & BOON®

*All the characters in this book have no existence outside the imagination
of the author, and have no relation whatsoever to anyone bearing the
same name or names. They are not even distantly inspired by any
individual known or unknown to the author, and all the incidents are
pure invention.*

*First published in Great Britain 2003
Harlequin Mills & Boon Limited,
Eton House, 18-24 Paradise Road, Richmond, Surrey TW9 1SR*

© Leah Martyn 2003

ISBN 0 263 83489 1

*Set in Times Roman 10½ on 12pt.
03-1203-43388*

*Printed and bound in Spain
by Litografía Rosés, S.A., Barcelona*

CHAPTER ONE

THE sky was a relentless blue again.

Liam Donovan stood on his verandah and looked out to where the river should have been. The riverbed was now almost dry. But still the waterbirds lingered hopefully each day in the late afternoon, their long bills seeking moisture from the sludgy-brown trickle.

Liam's broad shoulders lifted and he grated a rough sigh between his teeth. Parts of Australia were experiencing the worst drought for many years. And Wirilda, his part of the country, seemed to be suffering along with every other region of western Queensland.

Leaning over the timber decking, he emptied the dregs of his teamug onto the wildly flowering red bottle-brush. The hardiest of the natives, it simply produced more and more blossoms as if to defy the drought and the cruel grip it maintained on the land.

Going back inside to the kitchen, Liam glanced at his watch. It was still early, barely seven o'clock, but already the temperatures had begun climbing.

Thank God for the air-conditioning in his surgery. Because there was precious little else he could provide for his patients' well-being these days. Their depression, exhaustion and stress were being multiplied by the big dry.

And even though the drought hadn't actually killed

anyone yet, Liam knew the longer-term health of many of his patients on the land was in jeopardy.

And the effect of the drought didn't end there, he thought grimly. The shopkeepers and other small business operators in the town were being just as badly hit, when the district's primary producers were unable to spend.

It was a sobering thought. But unfortunately there was no magic prescription he could write that could take away their worries.

And it was frustrating him like hell.

Gathering up his breakfast dishes, he rinsed them and left them in the drainer. These days it was an extra chore but, like everyone else, he was prepared to do his bit. Severe water restrictions had been placed on the town and the use of dishwashers was definitely out.

Several minutes later, Liam hitched up his medical bag and slid his mobile phone into the back pocket of his chinos. Slamming the kitchen door behind him, he made his way through the small oasis of his court-yard garden to his garage.

He lifted his gaze, acknowledging the already hot bake of sun and feeling a curl of unease. The smell of smoke was in the air today. His expression tight-ened. That was all the district needed—bloody great bushfires all over the place!

In one swift movement he sent up the roller door on the garage. Striding into the space beyond, he unlocked his dark blue Land Rover and slid inside. He'd do an early hospital round first and then make his way across to his surgery in the town proper.

As he drove, he realised that on a professional

level things were getting desperate. He needed a competent partner like yesterday. But his search for a replacement for David Costigan, the GP he'd worked with for the past two years, was proving hopeless.

Impatiently, he lifted his hand from the steering-wheel, pushing his fingers through his thick dark hair. He couldn't blame Dave and Lizzie for baling out and moving back to the city. They'd quite rightly wanted better schooling opportunities for their teen-age kids, more options.

But that had left *him* the sole general practitioner for the district, with the nearest large medical facility nearly two hundred kilometres away.

Liam managed a sound halfway between a snort and a mirthless laugh. Perhaps, after all, he *was* being too picky, as Grace Chalmers, his practice manager, had rather pithily suggested yesterday. But he wasn't about to settle for just anyone to fill the gap. He had to be sure his final selection would want to dig in for the long haul. He owed that much to his patients.

Pulling into the forecourt of the small bush hospital, Liam cut the engine, swinging effortlessly out of his four-wheel-drive and making his way up the ramp to Reception.

'Hi, there, Liam.' Anna Marshall, the charge sister, was just coming out of her office.

'Morning, Anna.' Liam drummed his fingers in a little rat-a-tat on the counter top. 'Just checking on Sally Logan. What kind of night did she have?'

'Fairly good.' The charge proffered the file. 'And the bub seems to be settling well.'

Liam ran his eyes over his patient's chart. She'd

given birth to her first child two days ago and was urging Liam to let her go home.

But home was seventy kilometres away and there was no one, apart from her husband Ben, to give Sally any kind of support when she got there.

'I'll pop in on her now.' Liam returned the file with a brief smile. 'Has she had breakfast yet?'

'Just about to, I think. You've got a few minutes. Want me to come with you?'

Liam flicked a hand in dismissal. 'I think I can find my way,' he said drily. With swift strides he made his way along the short stretch of corridor to the two-bed unit. Tapping on the door, he poked his head in. 'Are you decent, Sally?'

'Oh, Dr Donovan!' Sally's eyes lit up. 'Come on in.'

The new mother was sitting up in bed nursing her baby daughter.

'You seem to have the knack of that quite nicely.' Liam's gaze was soft as he stood, arms folded, at the end of the bed.

The young mother husked a low laugh. 'She's a bossy little thing. She knew what to do from the start.'

'Feminine intuition, mmm?' Liam spun out a chair and lowered himself, leaning forward to clasp his hands between his knees. After a minute, he said, 'You know, Sally, even though things are going well with you and your baby, I'd like you to have a few more days with us.'

Sally made a small face. 'I really need to get back to Birra Birra, Liam. There's no one else to help Ben. I mean, at least I could be there to get his meals.

He's working from daylight to dark just now, pushing over scrub in a last resort to feed the cattle.'

Liam's heart went out to the young couple. Their whole livelihood was tied up in the land they were trying to farm. And it was obvious they had no extra money to buy additional feed for their stock. 'I wonder…?' He sat back in his chair and scraped a hand thoughtfully along his jaw.

'Wonder what?' Sally's blue eyes widened in query.

'As a compromise, whether you could give yourself two more days with us?' he asked bluntly. 'That way, with Anna's help you could get organised into a routine with the baby. Plus, I'd like you to have some gentle physio and massage before you go.'

The young mother coloured faintly. 'It's nice of you to suggest it, Liam, but we can't afford a physiotherapist.'

'It's all part of the service for first-time mums, Sally.' Liam mentally shrugged away the small untruth. 'You'd find great benefit from some appropriate exercises and you'll be able to do them at home as well.'

'Well…if you think I should…' Sally eased her daughter from her breast and kissed the top of her head.

'May I?' Liam offered gently, holding out his arms for the infant. 'Do you and Ben have a name yet for this new little person?' He stood, his large hands easily cradling the child, before he bent to tuck her back in her crib.

'We've decided to call her Amy.' Tenting her

knees under the sheet, Sally linked her arms around them. 'It means "beloved" and she's certainly that.'

Liam felt his throat tighten, as he looked down at the little one's breathtaking perfection.

That he should ever be so lucky…

He felt the oddest dip in his stomach as he stretched out his index finger to stroke the sweet curve of Amy's plump little cheek. Good grief! What was the matter with him?

He dragged in a much-needed lungful of air to dissipate the rush of emotion, spinning around to scoop up his chair and place it back against the wall.

'So, Mrs Logan.' He turned, propping his elbows on the traymobile at the end of the bed and raising a dark brow hopefully. 'Do we have a deal?'

'I…guess so.' Sally's pretty mouth tilted in a wry smile. 'I can see I'll be more help to Ben if I'm not falling in a heap when I get home.'

'Sensible girl,' Liam approved. 'Ah, that sounds like breakfast so I'll leave you to it.' He moved to the door and looked back with a wicked wink. 'Don't spend the day shopping now.'

Sally giggled. 'As if!'

Anna was just putting the phone down when Liam made his way back to the nurses' station. Seeing her rather strained expression, he asked abruptly, 'Anything I should know about?'

The charge nurse shrugged. 'That was my sister, Josie. It looks like she and Angus are going to have to up stakes.'

'Leave Bilbah Downs?' Liam's voice flew up several shocked octaves. 'But it's their whole life!'

'But not their livelihood any more.' Anna's mouth turned down. 'Josie said Angus has already sent their breeding stock to agistment, so at least they'll be fed even though it's an extra expense, and they'll have to sell the rest—not that they'll get much for them with the present glut on the market.'

Liam shook his head. Angus Sinclair was one of the district's most successful graziers. If he couldn't hold on, what hope did the rest of them have? He frowned heavily. 'Surely they'll come back?'

'If and when we get rain.' Anna shrugged. 'Meanwhile, they'll have to go elsewhere to earn a dollar. They've kids at boarding school with a mountain of fees a horse couldn't jump over.'

Sweet God. Liam felt the knot in his gut tighten. Was there to be no end to it? He lifted a hand and made a wiping motion over his cheekbones. 'I'm really sorry to hear all this, Anna. Is there anything at all I can do?'

'Oh, Liam…' Anna palmed the sudden wetness away from her eyes. 'You're already carrying the weight of the district on your shoulders…'

He gave a twisted smile. 'Lucky they're broad then, mmm?'

Anna hiccuped a laugh and desperately sought for composure. 'Sorry for losing it and inflicting my family's troubles on you,' she apologised quietly. 'Do you have some instructions about Sally?'

'Ah…yes.' Liam flipped his pen from his top pocket. 'Could you arrange with Lynn Poulson to give Sally some postpartum physio, please? I want her to have the works and ask Lynn to send the bill to my surgery.'

Which meant he'd pay for Sally's physiotherapy himself. Anna shrugged inwardly. It wasn't the first time Liam had done such a thing and she knew better than to comment. 'Fine. Anything else?'

'Sally's agreed to stay until Saturday so I'd be grateful if you'd give her as much practical help and advice as you can about managing herself and the baby. She's going to have to hit the ground running when she gets home.'

Somehow he had to keep positive.

Liam turned his vehicle in a swift arc and headed out of the hospital precincts. Everywhere he looked, the landscape was brown. Wirilda's winter had been harsh and long, and with no spring rainfall the pastures had had no chance to rejuvenate.

He grimaced. The logical part of his brain was consoling him that he could only do what he could do. But in the present circumstances, how could that ever be enough?

His surgery was in the centre of town. And there was only one thought occupying his mind as he coasted to a halt in the carport at the side of the building.

He had to find another doctor.

He couldn't go on trying to be confessor, counsellor and everything in between to his patients. He'd finish up being of no use to anyone.

In a decisive movement, he leaned over and heaved his bag off the passenger seat. Swinging out of the Land Rover, he made his way swiftly up the ramp at the front of the surgery, grunting a greeting to Grace as he went through to his consulting room.

'Good morning, Liam,' Grace said sweetly to the empty space, her raised eyebrows speaking volumes. Methodically, she turned and went into the kitchenette adjoining Reception. Several minutes later, she knocked on his door and went in.

'Energy boost for you,' she said, placing the tray with its mug of tea and chocolate muffin on his desk.

Liam turned from the window and rolled his eyes in resignation.

Grace sent him a reproving look. 'It's time to stop procrastinating, Liam. This place needs another doctor. I've brought the file with me. You're just going to have to decide on someone. Oh, and there was a phone enquiry this morning about the position as well.' Settling herself purposefully in the chair beside his desk, she opened the blue manila folder.

Liam gave a weary chuckle and threw himself into his chair. 'You're not about to let me off the hook, are you?'

Grace looked at him over the rims of her smart rectangular glasses. 'Not a chance. You're under tremendous pressure, Liam, and frankly not very nice to work with these days.'

'Not going to leave me, are you, Gracie?' He picked up his tea and took a careful mouthful.

'Don't be ridiculous.' Grace straightened the collar on her white shirt. 'I like my job. Most of the time,' she added darkly.

'These are good.' Liam sidetracked skilfully, biting into his muffin with obvious enjoyment. 'Did you make them?'

'I wish!' Grace cackled. 'You know I'm a hopeless cook. No, I thought we'd better buy whatever we can from the bakery at the moment—not that the sale of two chocolate muffins is going to save the Mandersons from bankruptcy.'

Liam's mouth compressed. 'Well, as the saying goes, every bit helps.' He picked up his mug and began draining it slowly. 'Leave the file with me. I'll go through it and make a short-list today.'

Grace looked sceptical. 'You promise?'

A sudden gleam of amusement lit his dark eyes. 'Count on it. Otherwise, I can see I'll have to bring in my whip and chair to defend myself. Seriously, I'd already made the decision to take some positive action. Now, you mentioned a phone enquiry?'

'Yes.' Grace began to pull the single sheet of paper from the back of the file. 'I jotted down the few details she gave me. Here you are. She's presently working in a group practice on the Gold Coast.'

'Thanks.' Liam's eyes went to the sheet of paper in front of him. 'What the hell…?' Suddenly his glance shot up, a stark look of disbelief crossing his face 'This one definitely *won't* do!'

Grace pulled back, making a tsk of annoyance. 'Why, for heaven's sake? Are we discriminating against women now?'

Liam propped himself forward, shielding his expression. He squeezed his eyes shut, seeing a halo of dark hair, grey eyes that were deeply beautiful, glinting to silver when she laughed, a full mouth, so vulnerable, so gentle when she slept…

'Liam?' Grace's motherly instincts were roused. He looked dazed. 'Is something—? Do you know this person?'

'You could say that…' The words came out throatily. 'She's my former *wife.*'

'Oh.' Grace waited out the few tense seconds that followed and then rose, closing the door quietly behind her.

Liam scrubbed a hand through his hair, conscious of his heart thrashing to a sickening rhythm inside his chest. After all this time. It was almost six years since they'd parted for crying out loud! His heart thumped again, while memories like a rusty merry-go-round cranked up and began turning slowly in his head.

So why now? The question pounded at him. Why?

On a growl of frustration, he reached out and snatched up the phone. There was only one way to find out.

Forcing his mind into neutral, he punched out the digits she'd provided, uncertain whether it was her work or after hours number. And did it matter anyway?

The number rang several times before it was answered. 'Southport Clinic. May I help you?'

Liam frowned down at the sheet of paper on his desk. 'Dr Nicola Donovan, please.'

There was hesitation briefly. 'We have a Dr Nicola *Barrett* on staff—'

Liam winced. Why hadn't he realised she would have changed back to her maiden name? The reality hurt. He didn't know why but it did. He gathered himself. 'May I speak to her, please?'

'She's just arrived. I'll put you through.'

Liam took a deep breath, feeling the swirl of mixed emotions well up like a balloon inside his chest, his nerves hanging by a thread, until she answered.

'Nicola Barrett.'

'What are you playing at, Nikki?'

'Liam—' A ripple of uneasy laughter followed. 'I never thought you'd call.'

'Well, I have. Now, what's going on?'

'I want the job at your surgery.'

Liam's mouth tightened. 'That's a ridiculous idea. And why would you bother, Nikki?'

'Perhaps I'm feeling altruistic.'

'Then give a donation to Care Australia.'

'I'll do that as well.' Nikki seemed unfazed. 'Liam, I've been watching the TV news each night seeing the effects of this terrible drought. You're obviously in desperate need of help or you wouldn't have advertised. Let me be the one. Please…'

Liam squeezed a hand across his eyes, already feeling his resolve weakening like ice under a blowtorch. Just the sound of her voice was turning his insides to mush… 'It'll be no picnic,' he warned. 'For starters, we've severe water restrictions in place.'

'So, no deep bubble baths, then?'

'No baths at all,' he countered. 'A three-minute shower is the order of the day.'

A beat of silence.

'Put you off, have I?' Liam's voice held the faintest thread of bitterness.

'Not at all. I was merely getting a mental picture of just how bad things must be out there.'

'You'd hate it,' he said flatly.

'Don't start making assumptions on my behalf, Liam,' she responded sharply.

'It would never work—'

'Why not? Unless… Are you with someone else these days?'

He drew in his breath so deeply it hurt. 'No. Are you?'

'No. So the timing couldn't be better, could it?'

'Nikki, if you've ideas of some kind of passionate reunion, forget it! If you come here, you come to work. And what about your present job? Are you intending to just chuck it in?'

'I'm here at Southport as a locum,' Nikki explained patiently. 'My contract finishes this week.' When it seemed as though he wouldn't be hurried into a decision, she added persuasively, 'Have you forgotten how well we work together?'

'I haven't forgotten anything about us, Nikki,' he answered roughly.

'So, doesn't it make sense to hire me?' she pressed earnestly. 'You wouldn't have to train someone up to speed. You can throw me in at the deep end and I'll swim.'

'Life in Wirilda is light years away from what *you*'re used to.'

'How do you know what I'm used to these days?' snapped Nikki, stung. 'I haven't exactly sat on my hands since we split up. Perhaps I should fax you the entire contents of my CV!'

'Calm down, Nikki. That's not necessary.'

'Well, then…?'

Liam's laugh was odd—a mixture of cynicism and

resignation. 'I'm just desperate enough to even consider this, and obviously mentally unsound. But all right. Consider yourself hired for the next three months and we'll see what shape we're in after that.'

'Thank you,' came the succinct response. 'Now, how do I get to Wirilda?'

Nikki put the phone down and realised her hand was shaking.

'I did it,' she said to the empty room, sudden tears filling her eyes and her voice barely a whisper, distorted by the tight little knot in her throat.

Reaction, she diagnosed, spinning off her chair and going to the water cooler in the corner. Holding the paper cup under the tap, she half filled it and then began sipping it in slow careful mouthfuls.

The conversation of the last few minutes seemed suddenly unreal. And she hadn't been ready for the way he'd sounded—so fed up, so under pressure. But he's stubborn, she told herself. Even with the dreadful conditions his patients must be facing, Liam wouldn't cave in.

He'll be fine, she told herself, and wondered why she was taking the state of Liam's welfare so much to heart. Anybody would think she was still in love with him, for heaven's sake! And how crazy was that? She was human enough to care—that was all…

'Liam…' She drew out her former husband's name on a quivery little breath and tried to remember the travel directions he'd given her.

She was to get a scheduled passenger flight from Brisbane to Longreach and then a Cessna six-seater would complete the journey to Wirilda. It flew out only once a week on a Tuesday. 'So, don't miss it, Nikki,' he'd warned. 'I'll be there to meet you at the strip.'

Suddenly, she felt all quivering nerve-ends as she returned to her desk and pulled the telephone directory towards her. She had flights to book. A new job to get her teeth into.

And an ex-husband to become reacquainted with.

CHAPTER TWO

LIAM felt as though his heart was jostling for space inside his chest. Surely the decision he'd made to let Nikki come here had to be bordering on some kind of masochism.

But it was too late to start having second thoughts now.

The Cessna had landed and the small group of passengers was spilling out through the door of the aircraft and down the narrow steps onto the dusty runway.

Liam moved closer. Where was she? Surely to heaven she'd hadn't slept in and missed the damned flight? Then he saw her. And out of nowhere desire flared. Emotions he'd thought long buried pushed to the surface like bubbles in a whirlpool, turning him inside out.

'Nikki!'

He watched her head come up, her shoulders straightening as if to resist the impact of his voice calling her name and felt a surge of regret for all the shattered dreams.

'Liam!'

Nikki's heart jerked alarmingly. He stood taller than anyone in the small group who'd gathered to meet the plane. And his fit, tanned leanness was apparent, emphasised by the snug-fitting white polo shirt and jungle green chinos.

But now she was almost up to him, she could see the fatigue of his eyes, the way the fine lines under his lower lashes looked so ingrained, as if carved there by the sharp tip of a scalpel.

The silence was absolute as they stood looking at one another. Nikki felt her composure flying every which way. Her professional detachment blown to smithereens. From beneath the cover of her eye-lashes, she allowed herself a further scrutiny of the man she'd once been married to. Her throat lumped. Would he reciprocate if she gave him a hug?

Probably not…

In a second, Liam had taken the decision right out of her hands. 'Welcome to Wirilda, Nikki,' he said gruffly, his smile faintly mocking.

He held out his hand towards her and slowly, re-luctantly almost, she placed her palm against his. His fingers curled around the back of her hand, his gaze sliding over her like a dark velvet caress. 'You've had your hair cut.'

'Ages ago.' Nikki laughed a bit stiltedly. Pulling her hand back, she lifted it in a defensive action to touch the edges of her jaunty little bob that just skimmed her ear lobes. 'I got tired of all that comb-ing and conditioning. This style is much more prac-tical.'

Liam was glad she hadn't asked if he liked it, be-cause he didn't. He'd loved her hair long, its dark strands over the pillow or slung around her shoulder in a silken, ebony twist. But even with her chic hair-style, she still looked impossibly young in her three-quarter pants, runners and hot pink T-shirt. He felt another glitch in his heartbeat.

'Do you have much luggage?'

Nikki slid her gaze away. 'Two suitcases. They're not huge.' She blocked a yawn. 'Sorry.' Her laugh was a trifle embarrassed. 'The flight left at five a.m. But we seemed to be ages getting here. I couldn't believe the stops we made.'

'It's a bit of a milk run.' Liam grinned but he looked guarded. 'I should've warned you.'

'Not to worry.' Nikki lifted a shoulder. 'Oh, that's my luggage Cliff's getting out now.'

Liam strode towards the rear of the plane not even the tiniest bit surprised she was already on first-name terms with the pilot. Out here, no one stood on ceremony. It was the nature of things in the bush.

He thanked Cliff Jameson and took charge of the two slightly battered suitcases. He felt vaguely surprised. In the old days Nikki would never have dreamed of owning anything but the most superior leather luggage.

But he gave the observation only fleeting interest and within a few minutes they were installed in his Land Rover. 'I imagine working here will be something of a culture shock for you,' he said with a stab of dark humour as they headed back along the ribbon of country road to the township.

Nikki moistened her lips. She could hardly believe she was here at all, let alone that he'd allowed her to come. 'Why would you think that?'

'Come on, Nikki...' Turning only his head, he eyed her broodingly.

She gusted a small sigh. 'If I say yes, will it make you happy, Liam?'

He didn't answer. Instead, he forced himself to

concentrate on the road. His thoughts were in turmoil. For two pins he'd turn around and put her back on the plane. It was never going to work—

'Where am I staying?'

'With me,' he said flatly, his jaw tightening. 'And I don't want an argument about it, Nikki.'

She pulled a face. 'I don't either. But is it wise?'

Liam gave a cracked laugh. 'If you're thinking people will gossip, forget it. At the moment everyone is just struggling to survive. The nature of our relationship will be the last thing on anyone's mind.'

Nikki digested that in silence and then said, 'I intend to pull my weight, Liam. I'll need a vehicle.'

'All arranged. We can lease one from the local garage. It'll be a smallish four-wheel-drive. Will that suit you?'

'And if I said no—' her tone was brittle '—what would you do?'

A thin smile edged his mouth. 'Don't waste your breath trying to wind me up, Nikki. I don't have any excess energy to fight with you.'

She averted her eyes quickly but not before he'd seen the pain in them.

'The flowering bottle-brush are really something, aren't they?' Nikki sent Liam a careful sideways glance, anxious to renew the conversation, to comment on anything that would help diffuse the gathering thickness of the atmosphere between them.

'Most of the trees seem to be surviving the dry remarkably well.' Liam lifted a hand from the wheel and dragged it back through his hair. 'Even the jacarandas have come into bloom.'

'You've jacarandas way out here?' Surprise edged Nikki's voice. 'That I must see.'

'You will.' His gaze softened for a second. 'There are a couple of old giants right in the centre of town. Someone with forethought or amazing optimism planted them years ago apparently.'

She laughed gently. 'Remember how they used to be in wild bloom all over the uni campus when we'd be preparing for our exams each year? And those little bell-like blossoms used to float down on us like confetti?'

'Mmm. The lawns looked for all the world like a lavender carpet...' The sudden reminiscing had made Liam's voice a bit throaty. 'Hell, life was simple then, wasn't it?'

'Compared with later—yes, it was.' Nikki's gaze became shuttered. Suddenly she sat upright in her seat. 'Liam! Slow down! Over there to your right—something untoward...'

'What the hell?' Automatically, he cut back his speed, guiding the vehicle over a rough shoulder of the road towards an adjoining paddock. 'Good grief—it's a car!' The metallic blue of the hood was now clearly visible, glinting in the hot morning sunlight. He frowned. 'It must've been travelling at speed to have broken through the fence like that.'

Nikki drew in a sharp breath. 'Looks like the driver's lost control and the car's catapulted down into the gully.'

'Whatever—well spotted, Nikki.' Liam swerved a burnt-out tree stump and brought the Land Rover to a juddering halt. 'We'll make a rural GP out of you yet!' He was already out of the car and pulling his bag from the back seat.

Nikki ignored the cynical little barb and scrambled out after him. This wasn't the time to get into word games with her ex-husband. She gritted her teeth, recalling how she'd casually mentioned something about jumping in at the deep end. Well, without doubt the deep end had materialised and she was barely off the plane.

Amazingly, the car had landed right side up but its bodywork had taken a battering.

'Oh, good Lord!' Liam's shocked exclamation echoed in the hazy stillness. 'It's Michelle Simpson's car.' He began sliding down to the accident scene, his feet fighting for purchase on the tacky clay surface. 'She's a nurse at the hospital. Ambulance, Nikki!' Turning, Liam tossed his mobile phone up to her. 'Tell the base it's the road from the airfield and we're about five K's out of town. And make sure they know it's one of the nurses.'

Forcing herself to keep steady and focus, Nikki punched out the triple zero number. Her request for an ambulance delivered, she closed off the mobile and shoved it into her back pocket. 'They'll get one to us as soon as they can,' she called to Liam. 'I'm coming down.'

'Mind how you go, then. The surface is like butter.' With a final heave, Liam succeeded in wrenching the driver's door open.

'Michelle…' He carefully released the seat belt, addressing the slumped form of his patient. 'Can you hear me? It's Liam Donovan. You'll be OK. We'll have you out of here in no time.'

The young woman moaned.

Nikki crawled in from the passenger side. 'She's taken a heck of a whack to her temple.' She began smoothing Michelle's fair hair back from her forehead, while Liam checked her vital signs. 'How's it looking?'

'BP a hundred and ten over sixty, pulse a hundred.' His mouth drew in. 'Doesn't indicate bleeding, thank heavens. But she's got to be suffering from shock.'

Nikki brought her gaze up. 'Do you have normal saline with you?'

'Yep. But I'm a bit pushed for space here. Think you could get an IV in from your side?'

Their movements began dovetailing and soon they were working together as seamlessly as they always had. 'IV's in and holding,' Nikki said crisply. 'And that's the ambulance by the sound of it.'

The ambulance bumped across the paddock to the accident scene, the two officers alighting and jogging across to the gully to peer down.

'Hey, Doc.' It was the senior officer, Baz Inall. He frowned. 'That's Michelle Simpson's car, isn't it? The base just said it was one of the nurses. I never thought it'd be Michelle. She's been driving around the farm since she was a nipper. What do you reckon happened?'

'We'll have to wait until she comes round to ascertain that, mate.' Liam was brief. 'Meanwhile, I suggest we treat her as a potential spinal injury.'

'Understood.' Baz knew the voice of authority when he heard it. 'We'll assemble the spinal stretcher and be right back.'

Nikki pulled her head out of the car, calling, 'We'll need a hard collar as well, please.'

'Any sign of her coming round?' Liam's face appeared back inside the car on the driver's side.

'She's floating in and out.' Nikki's heart went out to the young woman. She looked so pale. 'Do you have any idea what might have happened, Liam?'

'Can't say for sure.' Liam rubbed a finger across the bridge of his nose.

'She wouldn't have had a seizure of some kind?'

'Unlikely. I've never treated her for anything along those lines. She works a permanent night duty roster. Perhaps she fell asleep at the wheel.'

'That's awful.' Nikki shook her head. 'Sounds like she's exhausted. Is it necessary for her to work nights?'

Liam looked grim. 'Obviously, at the moment it is. Like so many others, Michelle, and her husband Danny are trying to keep their property going. He's away sinking bores most of the day so Michelle has to do the feed drop for the cattle on the tractor. And when you've got four hundred head or more, the process takes a while.'

A small frown knotted Nikki's forehead. There were obviously going to be problems ahead for the Simpsons if Michelle was going to be incapacitated for a time.

The ambulance officers were back quickly with the stretcher and Liam took the opportunity to make swift introductions. 'Janelle Murphy and Baz Inall, meet Nicola Barrett. Nikki's just flown in this morning,' he elaborated. 'She's joining me at the practice.'

'G'day, Doc.' There was a smile in Baz's voice as

he shook Nikki's hand. 'The boss got you to work already, has he?'

'I've not so much as signed a contract,' Nikki joked. 'Anyway, pleased to meet you both.'

'Do you play sport at all?' Janelle's keen blue gaze flew over Nikki's neat figure and unfussy clothes. 'We desperately need players for our netball team.'

Nikki responded to the younger woman's candour and obvious enthusiasm with a smile. 'Sorry, I don't play netball but I enjoy the odd game of tennis—'

'Could we get on, please?' Liam broke in, his dark brows flexing in faint irritation.

Trained hands were soon lifting Michelle gently onto the stretcher.

'I was hoping she might have regained a bit of colour by now.' Liam lent his strength to help ease the stretcher up out of the gully and into the waiting ambulance.

Nikki's gaze flew up to meet his. 'Are you having second thoughts about whether she may be bleeding?'

'I'm reasonably certain she's not.' He gnawed thoughtfully at his bottom lip. 'Her tummy appears soft, which would seem to indicate no spleen damage. Still…'

'Let's be doubly cautious, then,' Nikki proposed practically. 'Put her on a heart monitor. I'll travel with her to the hospital. That way I can keep an eye on her.'

'OK, thanks.' Liam glanced at his watch and frowned. 'I'm due at the surgery—'

'Go.' Nikki flapped a hand at him. 'I'll follow with Michelle.'

'Call me when you're squared away.' He began tossing stuff back into his medical bag. 'I'll collect you and get you home. I've *really* thrown you in at the deep end, haven't I?' he tacked on gruffly.

Nikki's heart thumped. 'I'm here to work,' she reminded him.

'Mmm.' Liam's mouth crimped at the corners in a dry smile. 'But I figured you'd at least have today to settle in. On the other hand...' his eyes raked blatantly over her '...it felt kind of good to be working together again, didn't it?'

'Like old times.' Hastily, she dipped her head and swung into the ambulance. In fact, it had felt wonderful!

It took only a few minutes for the ambulance to get to the hospital. And if Anna Marshall was surprised at the accompanying doctor's informal garb, she didn't show it. 'Liam said you'd be arriving this morning,' she said, as they exchanged names and proceeded to follow the trolley along to the small resus room. 'But what a welcome for you,' she lamented.

'Anna, it's the nature of the job sometimes,' Nikki countered with professional briskness. 'I didn't come to Wirilda expecting to attend tea parties every second day.'

'That's a relief.' The charge nurse chuckled. 'Because they're a bit thin on the ground at the moment.'

Nikki's mouth turned up in a smile. 'Do you have a gown I could pop on?'

'Sure, but you'll swim in it,' Anna predicted. 'The only sterile ones are Liam's. But I'm sure we've some smaller ones in stock. I just haven't had a chance to dig them out yet.'

'No hurry.' Nikki went to the basin in the corner. 'Oh, Liam said there's a water crisis…' She looked questioningly back over her shoulder.

'Not where hygiene is concerned.' Anna plucked a faded blue gown from the pile. 'We have it trucked in for the hospital.'

A slight moan from the bed had them both turning. 'She's coming round.' There was relief in Anna's voice. 'Mish…honey, you're in hospital.' She took Michelle's hand and squeezed. 'The new doctor's here. You'll be OK.'

Gowned and having thoroughly washed her hands, Nikki moved across to the treatment couch. 'Hello, Michelle.' She smiled. 'In case you don't remember, I travelled with you in the ambulance. I'm Nicola Barrett,' she added courteously, lifting her patient's wrist and looking down at her watch to check the injured nurse's pulse.

'On the whole, you've been pretty fortunate, Michelle.' Nikki's examination had been gentle but thorough. 'You'll have a thumping great bruise from the impact of your seat belt but you seem to have escaped any spleen damage.'

'I ache all over…'

'That's understandable. Let's check your legs and feet now for any deficits. Good, that's fine.' Nikki paused with her hand on the end of the bed. 'Be prepared for some residual whiplash in the next twenty-four hours. I'll put you down for Nurofen as a precaution.'

'You're keeping me in?' Michelle's voice rose in distress.

'Probably just overnight for observation. You've been concussed.'

'But I have to get home! Danny depends on me to feed the cattle…' She stopped and bit her lips tightly together.

Nikki pulled up a stool and sat down next to her patient. She didn't want to add to the young woman's troubles but obviously there was some sorting out to be done. 'Do you remember what happened?' she asked gently.

Michelle blinked confusedly. 'I must have fallen asleep. I came off duty at seven-thirty but I waited in town for the shops to open. I needed some groceries…'

'And then you tried to drive home?'

Michelle nodded.

'You don't think you fainted?'

'I know what you're asking, Doctor, but I'm not pregnant. I only wish I was…' Michelle's composure began to crumple. 'The way things are going, it'll be years before we can afford a family.'

Mentally, Nikki stepped back. There were a whole lot of separate issues here and emotionally Michelle was very near the edge. Nikki wasn't about to play the heavy doctor and insist on her admission.

'Perhaps we can do a deal here,' she said, deliberately infusing lightness into her manner. 'If you agree to take it easy and rest here until this afternoon so Anna can keep an eye on you, I promise if there's nothing of concern presenting I'll let you go home.'

'Oh. Thank you.' Michelle's eyes filled. 'I promise I'll rest quietly.'

'And I want you to take a couple of days' leave.'

'If only…'

'Michelle, I'm serious about this.'

Michelle swallowed. 'OK, I've a few days owing…' She managed a wobbly smile. 'I guess nurses are just the worst patients, aren't they?'

Nikki huffed. 'Try doctors. They're the absolute pits.'

'Tell me about it.' Michelle began to relax visibly. 'I've nursed a few in my time.'

Nikki made her way back to the nurses' station to fill Anna in about what she'd decided. She passed Michelle's chart across. 'Neuro obs for the next little while, please, Anna. I'm not expecting trouble but we certainly can't be too careful. And it would be helpful if Michelle could get some natural sleep.'

'I'll have her moved out onto the veranda ward.' Anna said. 'It's cooler and very quiet.'

'And I need to contact her husband…' Nikki tapped a finger thoughtfully across her chin. 'I imagine you have a number on file.'

'A mobile,' Anna confirmed with a little nod. 'I'll just bring it up on the computer for you.'

Nikki parked her elbows on the counter top. 'From what Michelle indicated, he'll have to come back early from wherever he's working and do her chores.'

'It won't be a problem. Danny's a nice guy. Naturally, he'll be upset about Michelle's mishap but on the other hand they're both sensible enough to realise in times like this the animals will have to come first. Now, what about you?' Anna raised a well-shaped eyebrow. 'I'll bet you could do with a cup of tea.'

Nikki laughed and put a hand to her heart. 'It would probably save my life, Anna. Thank you.'

The charge nurse tutted. 'Can't have you falling over on your first day.' She began ushering Nikki through to Sister's office. 'You can make your call from here. And while you're doing that, I'll away and see what I can rustle up from the kitchen.'

'Don't go to any trouble.'

'Rubbish,' Anna said mildly. 'Won't be a tick.'

'Bring an extra cup?'

'Will do.' Anna laughed her delight. 'I'm sure I can squirrel away a few minutes for a natter.'

Nikki made a small face as she put the phone down a couple of minutes later. The signal to Danny Simpson's mobile had been dodgy to say the least, but she'd more or less got the crux of her message through. Raising her arms to half-mast, she stretched and with a little sigh moved across to the big picture window.

Had she done the right thing in coming here? She tried to dampen the panicky feeling that had come out of nowhere. And the landscape was certainly doing nothing to lift her spirits, she thought, looking out at the drought-bare branches of several big trees etched like a child's stick drawings against the endless blue sky.

Perhaps the oddness of her mood was merely down to seeing Liam again and how it had affected her? She tamped down her apprehension. Allowing her thoughts to drift in *that* direction would do no good whatsoever. She couldn't allow herself to go there. Not yet…

'Here we are,' Anna announced cheerfully. 'Toasted sandwiches and a pot of tea.'

'Nothing like a good old brew, is there?' Nikki said a bit later.

'It's heaven, isn't it? Even on a hot day.' The two women had settled companionably over their second cup. 'So, how come you felt the need to work right out here in the sticks?' Anna asked with her usual frankness.

Nikki felt goose-bumps break out all over her. How much or how little to tell? She was no good at prevaricating. She'd be bound to forget what she'd said in the first place anyway. And wasn't there a saying that the truth always set you free? She moistened her lips. 'Liam and I go back a long way. I…heard he was facing rather desperate times with the drought and so on.'

'And you decided to lend a hand.' Anna smiled ingenuously. 'I think that's wonderful. It's certainly not easy for any of us here at the moment. But it's a very welcoming community, Nikki. You won't feel an outsider for long.'

CHAPTER THREE

SOMETHING was different about her.

Liam stared at the X-ray he was viewing, deciding it may as well have been a pig's trotter instead of his human patient's foot for all the sense it was making.

He made a sound of self-disgust as he peeled the negative off the screen, relieved he'd been focused enough to at least ascertain Jack Yardley had no broken bones. Still, the injury would keep the young stockman a bit quiet for the next little while.

Nikki. There she was again in his head. Against everything he was telling himself, his body tautened, desire as old as time stabbing him.

Damn her! No, damn himself. He'd been a monumental fool for letting her come here. He slammed the filing drawers shut and locked them, as if the action alone would negate the hunger stalking his loins—hunger only *she* could assuage.

He turned his head up, his short, sharp expletive hitting the ceiling. As if she was about to let *him* anywhere near her—

'Yes?' He turned abruptly at the knock on his door.

'Hi.' Nikki popped her head in and blinked a bit uncertainly. 'Grace said you'd finished…'

'Just now,' he countered gruffly. 'I was about to leave for the hospital to collect you.'

She raised an eyebrow. 'Well, as you see, I've saved you the trouble. Anna pointed me in the general direction of the garage so I went along and made myself known to Wayne Cassidy. He was very obliging and I'm now in possession of my fancy little Jeep.'

'Well, you never lacked initiative,' Liam growled, smiling crookedly.

Except when it came to hanging onto her marriage. Her mouth dried.

'You OK?' Liam's gaze ran clinically over her.

'Fine,' she lied, shaken to the back teeth at just being in the same room with him. In a little act of bravado, she moved closer and perched on the edge of his desk.

He looked moodily at her. 'How's Michelle?'

She told him, and that she'd managed to contact Danny Simpson.

Liam bent and fiddled with some paperwork on his desk. 'I've been in contact with the police. They've arranged for the car to be towed to the garage. It'll need panelbeating but otherwise seems OK. Wayne should have it back on the road fairly quickly for them.'

'Michelle mentioned she'd bought groceries— they're probably in the boot. There could be frozen stuff—'

'All taken care of.' Liam said, raising his eyes to hers. Something deep and dark shifted in them, and then he lifted a shoulder in a quick, dismissive action. 'The sergeant said he'd drop them off at the hospital kitchen. Danny can pick them up when he collects Michelle.'

'So, we're all squared away, then.'

'Seems like it.' Liam considered his fingertips for a minute. 'Thanks again, Nikki. Your help this morning was invaluable.'

Nikki looked away, choking on her feelings. 'Glad I seem to have your approval about something,' she offloaded jerkily, and slid to her feet. 'If you're through here, Liam, perhaps you wouldn't mind showing me the way home now?'

They arrived at Liam's place, which Nikki observed was modest, low-set and built of timber like most of the dwellings in the township.

'I don't have a lot of money to spare for luxury housing, Nikki,' he drawled, watching her gaze fly over the simple furnishings. 'But, then, I never did, did I?'

Nikki ignored the stark little reminder. These days she couldn't have given a toss about money. Having access to loads of it certainly hadn't helped their fledgling marriage stay on its feet... 'It's a nice house,' she countered. 'And I love the verandahs.'

'You're in here,' he said abruptly, opening the door on the front bedroom and carrying her luggage inside.

The room was unmistakably his. Nikki's anguished gaze darted from the bed, a serviceable king-sized ensemble, and back to Liam's closed expression. 'But this is your room.'

'I can doss anywhere,' he dismissed. 'You're not acclimatised yet, Nikki, and this is the only bedroom with air-conditioning. And if you can't sleep,' he rationalised, 'you won't be much use to me at the surgery, will you?'

Nikki covered the roughness of his remark with an over-bright smile. 'Well, at least you seem to have the message that I'm here to work.' She lifted a hand, her fingers plucking at the ribbed neckline of her T-shirt. 'It all looks very comfortable.'

'Sorry, I didn't have time to make the bed,' he apologised gruffly. 'There are sheets and stuff in the hall closet next to the bathroom.'

Nikki bit her lip, staring at the thrown-back covers, the mind-blowing thought striking her that she wouldn't have minded climbing into Liam's bed just the way it was. And where on earth did she think she was going with *that* scenario?

Unfolding her clenched hands, she held her palms against tops of her thighs. 'Thanks. I'm sure I'll find everything.'

A beat of silence.

'Hell…' Liam pressed his fingertips against his eyes and then scrubbed them over his cheekbones. 'This feels about as unnatural as trying to knit with toothpicks.'

'What does?' Her heart kicked and she swallowed.

'You and me,' he said, his eyes tangling with hers, 'standing here discussing sleeping arrangements as though we were never more than *friends*.' He gave a bleak smile. 'Does the wanting ever stop, Nik…?'

His throaty question sent her composure sliding every which way. She bit down on her bottom lip, recognising sickeningly the sweep of white-hot desire that ran through her. And suddenly she felt terribly afraid.

Afraid they were about to hurt each other all over again.

A rusty miaow at the door had them both turning. A large, beautifully striped tabby sat looking at them with an unblinking green stare.

'Oh—who's this?' Nikki laughed off-key, feeling a surge of gratitude towards the silly puss for giving them a chance to break the crippling tension. She swooped on the animal like a long-lost friend, stroking its back and petting it under the chin.

'That's Lightning.' Watching her, Liam's look was half-amused. 'He found his way here when he was not much more than a kitten. He'd been drenched in a storm.'

'Hence the name, I guess.' Nikki straightened, while the cat contented himself by rubbing against her leg and purring softly.

'Well, he seems to have taken to you,' Liam observed with a crooked grin. 'Turned traitor on me, have you, sunshine?' He playfully rubbed Lightning's tummy with the toe of his shoe and the cat miaowed again. 'He's probably hungry. He didn't show up for his food this morning. Come on, puss.' Liam led the way out into the hallway. 'Let's get you fed.'

Not quite knowing what else to do, Nikki followed man and beast through to the kitchen.

'Now, this had better hold you, sport, because it's all you're getting today,' Liam growled half-indulgently, proceeding to open a can of pet food. He tumbled the contents into the cat's dish and set it gently on the floor. 'You're a great boy, aren't you?' he murmured, scraping the animal between its ears with his thumb.

Nikki's hand went to her throat as memories as sharp as glass rose up to taunt her. 'You really missed your animals when we went to live in that ridiculous penthouse my father insisted on buying, didn't you?'

'I wanted to please you,' Liam murmured, 'and you wanted to please your father.'

Their eyes met and locked and she was trapped by the residue of tender regret in those dark depths.

She shook her head, as if something had just occurred to her. 'I should have supported you against my father's arrogance. But I honestly thought he knew best…'

Liam gave a hollow laugh. 'You were young, Nikki, conditioned to expect the best money could buy. While I…' He laughed again, a short, humourless sound. 'Let's just say we came from different worlds. And it all happened a lifetime ago.'

Nikki couldn't sleep. The bed was strange, the room unfamiliar, the absolute quiet, instead of relaxing her, had only succeeded in unnerving her.

There was no hum of traffic to provide a comforting background of a world going about its business, just the blur of the cicadas drumming outside her window and the occasional mournful howl of a dingo.

And as if that wasn't enough, the whole essence of Liam was in the bedroom. Haunting her. Even the scent of him was on the pillow, a scent she hadn't forgotten in all the months they'd been apart.

Hugging the pillow to her, she began wallowing in memories as sensual as the lingering fragrance of his skin.

She sniffed. Damn. Her cheeks were wet and there was something wrong with her chest, as if an elephant had placed its huge weight there.

The sob hiccuped its way out, and she turned into the pillow, smothering the agonised sound as it squeezed from her throat. Oh, Lord, what if Liam had heard?

She finally slept, rising early next morning and realising she felt better, more in control.

And under the needling heat of the shower, even a three-minute one, she felt her body revive.

Dressed for work, she made her way along to the kitchen, surprised that Liam hadn't surfaced yet. She gave an inward shrug. She'd get on with making breakfast. He was bound to turn up sooner or later.

Her gaze ranged around the homely room, lighting on the worn pine table on which sat a fruit bowl full of oranges and several stacks of medical journals.

Methodically, she set places for them both and then unearthed a black and white butcher's apron from a hook behind the door. An impish smile lit her mouth as she wound the apron around her and tied the strings.

'Well, look at you, Dr Barrett…'

Nikki spun round from the cook-top and shot her former husband a haughty little look. 'Good morning. I thought I'd get breakfast started.'

'I'm gobsmacked.' Arms folded, Liam lent indolently against the doorframe, watching her. 'I can't believe what I'm seeing.' His eyes held laughing dis-belief. 'You cooking *anything*!'

Nikki did her best to ignore his banter. 'There's some freshly squeezed orange juice and I found some English-type muffins in the freezer. I'm toasting them under the grill. Would you like scrambled eggs to go with them?'

'Sounds terrific.' He'd pushed himself away from the door and moved across the kitchen to look over her shoulder. 'Like me to crack the eggs?' His voice was gruff, his hand of its own accord coming up to rest absently at the nape of her neck.

Nikki felt her adrenalin levels surge with alarm and turned her head a fraction. He was there, hov-ering on the edge of her vision. Her nostrils thinned and she breathed in his maleness. His nearness. 'Ah…yes, please,' she said hastily. 'Do you still pre-fer tea in the morning?'

'I never drink coffee.' He dropped his hand and moved away. 'You should remember that, Nikki.'

'Well, I've changed in lots of ways,' she justified airily, rescuing the toasted muffins and placing them on a warming tray. 'I thought perhaps you had as well.'

His chuckle was a bit rusty. 'Perhaps I have. We'll just have to wait and see, won't we?'

Nikki felt a curious swirl of pleasure watching Liam obviously enjoy the simple meal she'd pre-pared. Busying herself pouring the tea, she asked, 'So, what kinds of cases can I expect in my surgery today?'

'What kinds of cases?' Over the rim of his teamug, Liam sneaked a glance at her clear, olive complexion, untouched by make-up. She still looked not much older than the twenty-year-old he'd met for the first time in the medical library at the university all those years ago. Very deliberately, he took a mouthful of his tea. 'How are your counselling skills?'

She smiled, activating the tiny dimple in her cheek. 'Pretty good, even if I say so myself.' And then she sobered. 'I expect you're seeing patients who have come in with an unexplained pain somewhere but in reality they really need to talk.'

'Exactly.' He gave a brief nod of approval at her grasp of things. 'You'll have patients coming in with physical ailments like muscular spasms, often neck and shoulder pains, that are purely manifestations of stress. Because many of them feel their livelihoods are in jeopardy, they're quite unable to wind down and relax.'

'So, blood-pressure problems presenting as a result?' Nikki surmised.

'Mmm.' Liam set his mug down with exaggerated care, and wrapped his hands around it. 'And not just BP problems. I have several patients who need referral but they don't want to be away from their farms just now.'

Nikki's mouth pulled down. 'In other words, they're just soldiering on.' She shook her head. 'They must feel as though their lives have been turned inside out.'

Watching her, Liam felt a thread of unease. She'd always had such a tender heart about her patients. Had he been the biggest fool to have let her come here in these troubled times? 'You can't wear their stress, Nikki,' he warned. 'You prescribe where necessary and listen only.'

She sent him an old-fashioned look. 'Do you mean to sit there, Liam Donovan, and try to tell me *you* don't get involved with your patients' problems?'

'All right.' He held up a hand in mock surrender. 'Here and there, I suppose.'

'Of course you do,' she said softly, and felt her heart lurch painfully. The way he practised medicine, his caring, was one of the many things she'd loved about him.

Promptly, at eight o'clock, Nikki presented herself at the surgery.

Grace was already in attendance and busily sorting through the patient files for the morning clinic when Nikki pushed her way in through the glass front door. They swapped a smile.

'My, don't you look smart!' Grace eyed Nikki's tailored long shorts and crisp lemon and white striped shirt with approval.

Nikki's hand went to the sweep of bare skin revealed by the turn-back collar. 'It's not too...?'

'Informal?'

Nikki chuckled. 'I was going to say revealing.'

'Don't be silly!' Grace flapped a hand. 'You look...' She put her head on one side. 'Laid-back is the expression, I think. But businesslike as well.'

'Oh, good.' Nikki laughed a bit uneasily. 'I didn't want to come across as done up to the nines and unapproachable.'

'Oh, I don't think you could ever be like that,

Nikki,' Grace said kindly. 'You look perfectly groomed for Wirilda.'

Nikki rested her medical case on the counter top. 'Just don't ask me to wear a white coat.'

'As if!' Grace dismissed scornfully. 'They've long disappeared out of use in general practice. But Liam keeps a supply of theatre scrubs if you need to carry out any treatments.'

'Speaking of Liam.' Nikki glanced at the round-faced clock on the wall behind Grace. 'He's doing a hospital round and then he's on what he called his "outlying patient run". Round trip of two hundred K's—is that right?'

'Absolutely.' Grace nodded. 'That's why it's such a godsend to have another doctor, Nikki. Even in the short time you've been here, you can see the kind of workload he's been carrying.'

Nikki could indeed. 'So, how is my list for this morning looking?' She pulled the desk diary towards her.

'Pretty full. But the first one isn't due until eight-thirty. You've a few minutes to go over things. And there are a couple of X-rays that I've put with the relevant patients' files.'

Nikki nodded gratefully. 'Thanks, Grace. And I prefer to come out and call each patient in when it's their turn, if that's OK?'

Grace beamed. 'Liam likes to do that, too. I can see you working splendidly together.'

Well, they had—once. Nikki gave a trapped smile, before turning and making her way along the short corridor to the consulting room Liam had set aside for her.

Her first patient, Bernard Hardy, was right on time. 'Have a seat, Mr Hardy.' Nikki smiled. 'I'm Nicola Barrett.'

'Heard you'd arrived.' The middle-aged man sank onto the upright chair at right angles to Nikki's desk. 'And it's Bernie, Doc.' He gave the glimmer of a smile. 'Nobody around here would know who Mr Hardy was.'

'Bernie it is, then.' Nikki referred to the file on her desk. 'You've been to see Liam about long-term pain in your heel.'

'Had to have it X-rayed.' His throat rippled as he swallowed uncomfortably. 'Liam said to come in to-day for the result.'

Nikki tapped the large white envelope on her desk. 'I've had a look at your X-rays, Bernie. It's quite clear you've developed what's called a spur.'

'Thought there was something.' Bernie raised a hand to stroke his short dark beard. 'You don't get sharp pain like that for no reason. Could you explain what's caused it, Doc? So I can tell Meg—the wife,' he clarified with a lopsided grin.

'Well, it's a fairly common condition,' Nikki said, swinging to her feet. 'About one in five people de-velop a bony spur on the heel. Take a look at the X-ray with me.' Anticipating her patient would possibly want confirmation of the diagnosis, Nikki had al-ready clipped the film onto the screen.

'Hang on a minute, Doc.' Bernie fumbled his spec-tacles out of his shirt pocket and put them on.

Nikki showed him the outline of the spur. 'Now, what it does is press into the surrounding soft tissue, here and here. And that's the source of your pain.'

'Nasty-looking beggar,' he said consideringly, surveying the skeletal framework of his right foot. 'So, what do you now, Doc? Cut it out?'

'Nothing like that.' Nikki gave a quick smile. 'There are a couple of things we can try for starters, like alternating hot and cold foot soaks for ten minutes twice a day, then rolling the sore spot over a golf ball for about five minutes every hour.'

''Struth!' Bernie removed his glasses and placed them back in their case. 'That all sounds a bit weird—if you don't mind me saying so. How's rolling me foot over a golf ball goanna help exactly?'

'It will help to soften the tissue and break the painful spasm of the muscles and tendons on the foot.' Nikki flicked off the light on the screen. 'I'll give you a script for some painkillers as well. But be prepared, Bernie, it may not be a quick fix.' Nikki resumed her seat and pulled her prescription pad towards her. 'What kind of work do you do?'

Her patient folded his arms across his chest, as if settling in for a chat. 'I used to have a spraying and weed-control business. Had it for fifteen years. But now, with the drought...' He stopped and shook his head. 'Once upon a time I was flat out keeping up with the work the farmers wanted done. This winter I didn't get one spray job.'

Nikki's heart went out to her patient but recalling Liam's very definite advice, she merely sat and listened.

'Meg managed to get some cleaning work at the hotel so at least we can eat.' He laughed hollowly. 'I feel so bloody useless...'

Nikki felt quite choked. Blinking quickly, she

wrote the date across the top of the pad. 'Do you have children, Bernie?'

'Two boys.' He looked bleak for a second. 'Peter, the eldest, finishes high school this year. Looks like he'll have to go to the city for work. There's nothing here for him.'

'Well, perhaps not just at the moment.' Nikki tried to sound encouraging. 'But when we get rain, things will pick up.' She handed him the prescription. 'And look on the positive side. You need this time off work to get your foot working properly again, don't you?'

'Can't help feeling scared for the future, though.'

Nikki felt her throat dry. 'Well, that happens to most of us, Bernie—some time or another.' She got to her feet to see her patient to the door. 'Let me know how you get on with your treatment. No need to come in—just phone. I'll be here most days. Unless, of course, you'd like to stay as Liam's patient?'

'You'll do fine, Doc.' Bernie rubbed a hand across his cheekbones and looked faintly embarrassed. 'And, uh, thanks for listening, like…'

Nikki nodded. 'Any time.'

Blindly, she went back to her desk and sat there, gathering her thoughts. And coming to the unhappy conclusion that, without doubt, as the town's medical officers, she and Liam were going to see more and more patients suffering from post-traumatic stress syndrome for many months to come.

That's if she was still here, of course.

CHAPTER FOUR

'WHAT are you doing?'

Nikki spun her head round, feeling her heart bounce off her ribs. Liam was parked against the outdoor lattice screen, arms folded, watching her. 'I'm building a herb spiral.' Her voice was so small she could hardly hear it herself.

'A what?' His mouth twisted sardonically as he came towards her, hunkering down beside her, his face almost at her level.

Nikki felt suddenly self-conscious. She'd been in Wirilda nearly two weeks now and already his place felt like home. And if it was, then there were things she needed to be doing around it. But on the other hand, she didn't want to be seen as taking liberties.

She took a deep breath, catching the familiar scent of his aftershave. 'I got the plants and stuff from the nursery,' she explained hurriedly. 'You have so much under-utilised space around this courtyard, Liam. It seems a shame not to make the most of it.'

His mouth tucked in at the corners. 'There happens to be a water shortage as well. How do you propose keeping your plants alive?'

'Give me some credit.' She sent him a brief exasperated look. Did he think she'd just rushed out and bought things willy-nilly? 'For starters, we should be using grey water.'

'Recycled water?'

'That's another name for it, yes. One simple action like taking a plastic bucket into the shower with us would catch enough water to keep quite a large veg patch thriving.'

'On the other hand,' he said softly, 'if we showered together, that could in itself be quite a saving measure.'

Nikki's pulse thudded. He was jesting, of course, but she was in no mood to laugh. Instead, she pulled out all her mental reserves to halt the swarm of vivid memories his words had reignited. 'We lost those kinds of privileges when we divorced,' she snapped.

His eyes glinted and there was a brief, taut silence before he said mockingly, 'So, enlighten me.' He waved a hand over the little plants she'd assembled on the ground. 'How does this thing work?'

'Well, essentially, I'm planting my herbs into a cartwheel shape.' Nikki caught her lower lip between her teeth, concentrating on the simple practicalities. 'As the plants grow, they'll move towards its centre and climb around and up, forming a mound.'

His quizzical look told her he understood the basics of what she was saying. 'So, in reality, you're creating different micro-climates, is that it?'

She searched his face and then nodded. 'And I'll be able to suit each herb to the environment. The herbs that prefer moist conditions will go near the bottom of the spiral so they'll catch and retain the last dribble of water, and the hardy ones—'

'Will go on top of the spiral,' Liam finished for her. 'So, may I help, then? That way I'll feel as if I'm doing my bit towards saving the planet.'

Nikki's throat dried at the look of youthful enthusiasm on his face. 'Yes... I suppose.' She gave a stilted laugh, pulling her gaze away in an attempt to stifle the sudden drench of vulnerability.

They spent a companionable amount of time setting up the planting system. 'These will be best for the top,' Nikki said, separating the little pots to one side.

'So, what are we planting?' Liam's eyes narrowed over the labels. 'Garlic chives, oregano, rosemary and thyme.'

'And they're just for starters,' Nikki looked at him, her smile faintly wary. 'I've asked Pam at the garden centre to order in several more varieties. I want to try lavender as well.'

'No doubt she'll be glad of the extra business.' Liam picked up the trowel. 'So, we should start at the base and work up?'

Almost an hour later Nikki sat back on her heels and looked at their handiwork with a feeling of achievement. 'That was quite a big job.'

'And the most fun I've had in ages.'

Nikki raised an expressive eyebrow but refrained from comment. The fun, she realised, had been in doing the job together. She wondered if Liam recognised the fact.

There'd been something nostalgic and homely about the afternoon, Liam thought, watching Nikki trail her fingertips almost lovingly across the tiny just-planted seedlings, then turn to begin tidying the work space. Her dark head was at a pert angle, her movements neat and quick, so achingly familiar as she tossed the empty pots into a nearby carton.

'I'll get rid of that,' he offered in a curiously gruff

voice, hefting the carton and making his way towards the rubbish bin at the end of the yard.

'Don't throw the carton away,' she called after him.

'It'll break down on the compost heap.'

Liam half turned and saluted. He felt his gut tighten. She'd slipped back into his life almost seamlessly. And the fact was, it felt utterly right. And just where do you think you're going with that conclusion, Donovan? His jaw worked and almost savagely he began to tear the cardboard into large, unwieldy chunks.

Nikki watched him for a moment, a strange excitement filtering through her. Suddenly she turned away in an almost defiant gesture, stripping off her gardening gloves and snatching up the straw broom.

'What *is* this, Nikki?' Liam came up behind her, intercepting her almost manic sweeping with a firm grip on the handle of the broom. 'For heaven's sake!' He tossed the offending implement viciously aside. 'I don't expect you to work like a navvy while you're here!'

'I'm just finishing the job I started.' Nikki set her mouth, determinedly telling herself she wasn't feeling what she was faintly ashamed of feeling. That her former husband's closeness was making her sick with nerves. Vulnerable all over again. Exposed. She licked her lips and tried to ease her shoulders. Automatically, they tightened again as his gaze narrowed, and he lifted a hand to gently stroke her cheek with the tips of his fingers.

'You've managed a nice old smudge here…' The huskiness in his voice ran all over her bones, the trail of his fingers over her skin like live wires. She could hardly drag air into her lungs. Dizzily, she saw the misty sheen of sweat in the hollow of his throat and felt the controlled urgency in his every muscle. 'Nikki…?' He dropped his hand abruptly and caught her about the waist.

Her eyes dilated and she shivered beneath his touch. She swallowed thickly. 'What are you doing?'

'Just this,' he husked, gathering her in and cradling her against the solidness of his chest.

A brief whimper of disbelief escaped from her mouth and then her hands were sliding under his T-shirt until her arms were around him, anchoring him as if she'd never let him go.

He felt wonderful—sleek-muscled, so familiar. And she still knew his body as well as her own, her touch revelling in the feel of it under her hands.

But the urge to touch wasn't hers alone. Liam's hand slid from her shoulder to cup her breast and stroke the soft under-swell.

'Oh, Nik…' Her name was torn from his throat and lost against her lips, his mouth catching her own breathy sigh, swallowing it, savouring it, until he claimed her as though he was dying of thirst.

Then just as suddenly it was over. Like a fever that had run its course.

With one accord they stepped back from each other. For a few taut seconds their gazes held, then Liam squeezed his eyes shut briefly. 'We've done enough for today. Why don't you take the shower first?'

Nikki let her breath out slowly. Her first instinct had been to analyse what had just happened—the kiss and all it stood for. But obviously Liam was already sidestepping the issue. Or perhaps he intended to forget it had happened at all.

In a quick, protective movement, she put her hand to her mouth, feeling his kiss rebound in a wash of quivering nerve-ends.

If only it was that easy.

Nikki closed off the taps and stepped out of the shower, hastily drying herself. Winding a towel turban-like around her damp hair, she decided she'd just about got the three-minute routine down pat.

Opening the bathroom door cautiously, she called, 'Shower's free!' She heard the faint tremble in her voice as it echoed down the hallway and, almost as if she was being pursued, scuttled into her bedroom and closed the door.

'What about a glass of wine before we think about dinner?' Liam asked a bit later.

'Lovely.' Nikki had regained some sense of normality, settling herself at the servery with her elbows propped on the counter and her chin in her hands.

Watching her former husband move around the kitchen, her gaze was almost hungry. She knew all his features by heart—the coal-black eyes that seemed to see right to your soul, the hair, unruly still, springing back from his temples in a tangle of dark waves, the strength of his facial features, these days honed to an almost hawk-like leanness.

'Here you are, Doctor, a nice crisp Chardonnay.' Liam slid the drink across to her and their fingers brushed as she took it. She tensed, sharp bitter-sweet memories of their kiss enveloping her as the electric tingle shot up her arm and hovered around her heart.

'Shall we go outside to the cool?' Liam gestured towards the rear verandah and Nikki spun off the high stool and followed him.

It was early evening and a Sunday.

'It feels good to unwind a bit, doesn't it?' Legs outstretched, Liam's gaze narrowed on the long back yard, the straggly she-oaks at the end of it.

'Mmm.' Nikki made herself more comfortable in the canvas director's chair and placed her drink on the nearby low table. After a while, she remarked, 'We need some greenery out here, Liam. Some hanging baskets would be terrific, have such a cooling effect. I mentioned it to Pam. She's going to sort out some kind of hardy ferns for us.'

Us? Liam frowned. The inclusive pronoun had slipped so easily from her tongue, adding a dangerous dimension to the new kind of intimacy they seemed to have found.

Lifting his glass, he took a careful mouthful of his wine, a cross-current of apprehension zig-zagging up his backbone. His heart was still too battered to become involved again. And yet…was there anything he could do to stop it happening, even if he wanted to?

It was a long time before either of them spoke again and then it was to discuss what to have for dinner. 'A barbecue would be nice and easy.' Nikki tipped her head on one side and smiled at him hopefully.

'Except all outdoor fires are banned at the moment,' Liam countered.

Nikki raised an eyebrow. 'Take-way?'

But again he shook his head. 'There's still some of that chicken casserole left and we could do some jacket potatoes in the microwave.'

'Sounds good. And I'll make a green salad with everything in it to freshen our palates.' Nikki moved across to the fridge. The wine had begun to create a warm glow inside her and almost automatically her gaze drifted over her ex-husband as he busily scrubbed potatoes at the sink. Half closing her eyes, she absorbed his essence, letting her senses take over to run full pelt into the realms of forbidden territory.

Between them, the preparation of the food took little time and then they carried everything outside. 'A candle might be nice,' Nikki said almost shyly.

Liam pulled a face. 'OK. But not on the table. It'll draw the moths.'

Nikki felt her stomach knot. 'I won't bother, then.' She felt deflated. Obviously he thought she'd been trying to engender some romance into their evening. Feeling caught out in some way, she set the plates down with a little thump, the feeling of togetherness they'd experienced earlier gone like yesterday's tide.

'I'll make some tea, shall I?' Liam said when they'd finished eating, scowling down at his wineglass, which was still half-full. They'd struggled through the meal, with stilted comments about the practice, one or two of their patients, the chance of rain before Christmas…

Nikki nodded. 'Fine.'

But Liam made no effort to move. Instead, he felt his gaze drawn towards his former wife, to her bravely held little chin, the soft curve of her cheek, the sweet fullness of her mouth. His gaze lifted to her silver-grey eyes, so pale they were almost transparent. As though they were windows to what was going on in her mind.

'Don't look at me like that, Liam,' Nikki said awkwardly.

'Like what?'

She saw the swift jerk of his muscle as his jaw compressed. 'As though—as though you've never seen me before.'

'You're different somehow.'

'We're both older...' She swallowed uncomfortably.

He frowned. 'It's more than that. You've grown in ways I can't make out.'

'I've extended my horizons over the last few years. Something must have rubbed off.'

Liam shook his head. 'The way you've tackled things here. Fitted in, as though you were born to it. And all this stuff about the ecology...'

Her eyes flew up to meet his, the look in them sending her heart lurching sideways. 'It's just something I've been working on.'

'Where?'

Nikki rocked her hand dismissively. 'Here and there.'

'That's not an answer, Nikki.' His dark brows shot together. 'I could ask to see your CV,' he pointed out thinly.

'Oh, all right!' Unable to sustain the intensity of his gaze, she dipped her head. 'I've spent most of the past year and a half working for Médecins sans

Frontières, first in North Vietnam and more recently in Papua New Guinea.'

'Bloody hell.' His head came up sharply. 'I'd never have guessed. But it's fantastic you did something like that, Nik. I'm so proud of you.'

Her eyes flashed silver. 'I did it for me, Liam—not to impress you or anyone.'

His mouth drew in. 'Did your father approve?'

'No, he didn't! But I went anyway.' She swung to her feet, as if to close the subject. 'Now, are we going to make this tea or what?'

CHAPTER FIVE

ANOTHER week or so had passed. Nikki stood at her surgery window looking out, deciding she didn't know whether coming to Wirilda had been such a good idea after all.

She'd only meant to help Liam through a crisis. She certainly hadn't meant to begin chasing old shadows, opening old wounds. And yet that's exactly what she'd done. But then, Liam had done his share of chasing and opening, she reflected bleakly, her thoughts winging back to the previous evening.

The conversation had begun innocently enough. They'd done a late round at the hospital and then stopped off to buy fish and chips on the way home. Sitting over their informal supper, Nikki had said, 'Michelle came in for a final check-up today.'

Liam had raised a dark brow. 'How was she?'

'Everything was fine and she's cut back on her night shifts.'

'That's good. Danny seems a supportive partner. That will have helped.'

'Every marriage should have one,' Nikki had responded with an over-bright smile.

A beat of silence.

'Yes, they should.' He'd made a sound, half impatience, half sigh. 'That's where we fell down, wasn't it?'

She'd raised her head a fraction and met his eyes.

They'd been over-bright and a lump had risen in her throat. 'We can't go back,' she'd said softly.

'No.' He'd looked out into the soft night surrounding them. 'I should've tried harder.'

'*I* should've tried harder,' she'd countered, biting her lips and looking down at her hands. 'My father always got in the way. I can see that now.'

Liam had laughed hollowly. 'My family didn't have money. I was never going to be good enough for his daughter, was I?'

'Don't.' Nikki had looked away, choking on her feelings. Her father had been scathing about Liam and she'd been torn between the two.

Suddenly, the day of their parting was crystal clear in her mind. The day when Liam had come home from the Royal Brisbane where they'd both worked and had said flatly, 'There's no place for me here, Nikki. Your father's money bought this place. His influence is everywhere. It's like having a third person in our marriage. I'm jack of it. I'm leaving.'

Even though things between them had been tense for weeks, Nikki had been shocked almost beyond words. And then anger had taken over. How could he be so ungrateful? Her father had done so much for them. She'd said the first thing that had come into her head. 'You've never got rid of that great lump of wood off your shoulder, Liam. You've never even tried to fit in with my family's expectations! Instead, you expect me to live like some kind of…*peasant*! So, yes, go. Maybe that's the best thing for both of us.'

And, tight-lipped, he'd gone, just like that.

And she'd let him. And her father had rushed to

console her. 'Come home where you belong, Nicola. Divorce the young whippersnapper. And if thinks he'll come out of this marriage with any of my money, he can forget it. I made sure the property was in your name only.'

'Oh, dear God.' Nikki sighed, wrapping her arms around her midriff and turning away from the window. It was all so long ago and she'd been young and easily influenced. And Liam had been young and as stubborn as a mule.

Looking back, it was easier to see the mistakes they'd made. But, left to their own devices, perhaps they could have made a go of their marriage.

If only her father hadn't kept sticking his oar in.

Glancing down at her watch, she saw it was lunchtime. Liam would be waiting. They'd got into the habit of having a bite to eat and discussing their morning. Slowly, as if mentally she was wading through liquid concrete, she made her way across the corridor to the lunchroom.

While they were waiting for Grace to arrive with their usual pot of tea and sandwiches, Liam said, 'I've had two cases of toddlers presenting with vomiting and diarrhoea this morning. Both families are residents of the caravan park.'

Nikki raised an eyebrow. 'Is that significant?'

'It could be. Let me know if you strike any over the next day or so, please, Nikki.'

She nodded. 'Perhaps folk are being a bit lax about washing their hands, thinking they're saving water.'

'Maybe. Maybe not. It could be something else entirely.' He went quiet for a few seconds, then said,

'If any more kids go down, we'll have to act swiftly to trace the source.'

By the end of Nicola's afternoon surgery, Liam's worst fears had been realised. Nerissa Bycroft, the young mother of a toddler, James, was frantic with worry. 'He's vomiting everything, Doctor.'

Nikki examined the child carefully. He seemed exhausted, poor little pet. 'What are you giving James, Nerissa?'

'Not much—because he wouldn't take much. I tried him with a cup of milk and a bit of custard—he usually loves that.'

'And he threw it right back at you?' Gently, Nikki smoothed a twist of fair hair from the little boy's forehead.

The young mum looked uneasily at her son. 'I've stuffed up, haven't I? But I've had no one to ask.' She swallowed. 'We've come into town from one of the station properties. Jared, my husband, was working for the Sykes family at Torrington. But with the drought they've had to let him go.' She stopped and bit her lip. 'He's gone over the border to look for work in New South Wales.'

'And where are you living now, Nerissa?' Nikki asked, needing for everyone's benefit to get an overview of the family's situation.

The young woman looked glum. 'At the caravan park. The facilities are pretty basic and the manager is the pits. He's recently had all the vans connected to tank water and upped the charges. I complained and he told me if I didn't like it, there were plenty of people to take my place.'

'That sounds like intimidation!' Nikki's eyes

flashed in anger. 'Surely you should report him to the council?'

'No. I couldn't do that.' Nerissa's throat constricted. 'You won't say anything, will you, Dr Barrett? He'll chuck me out—and I've nowhere else to go with James.'

Nikki's mouth firmed. 'Of course I won't implicate you, Nerissa. But James is the third toddler from the park we've seen today with gastro symptoms. Something is amiss and as Health Officer for the district, Dr Donovan will have to report our findings to the council. For the moment, though, let's try to get this little one more comfortable, shall we?'

Almost on cue, as though to hurry things along, James began to whimper and pull his legs up as if in pain.

'Right.' Nikki pulled her pad towards her. 'Keep James right off milk for the moment, Nerissa. He should be having small, frequent amounts of clear fluids only.'

The young mum nodded. 'How small? And how frequent?'

'Good questions.' Nikki's mouth turned up in a brief smile. 'Small means about twenty mils. Do you have a measure at home?'

'I have a whisky measure. Will that do?'

'That's fine. Now, clear means not milk and not solids, just fluid. I'll give you a note for the chemist. He'll have various mixtures you can add to water. They're especially designed to replace all the water and chemicals little James may lose because of his continual vomiting.

'But if he rejects that, try diluted lemonade. Say

one part to four parts water. If you like, freeze it and make little ice cubes for him to suck.'

'I can do that.' Nerissa looked eager. 'So, how often?'

Nikki considered. 'Let's go with every fifteen minutes to start with and then you can lengthen it to thirty minutes if he's tolerating it and looking happier. We have to be aware of James dehydrating so if you're at all worried, ring me day or night or take him immediately to the hospital. Either Dr Donovan or I will be straight over.'

'Thank you so much, Dr Barrett.' Nerissa blinked fast as she struggled to her feet with the now-sleeping toddler. She put out a hand and took the script. 'I'll get started right away.'

Nikki went to open the door for her and then hesitated, disturbed by her train of thought. 'Use bottled water for the time being, Nerissa, and I'll call in at the park tomorrow and check James over.'

Nerissa bit the underside of her lip. 'I'd rather bring him here—if that's OK?'

Sensing the girl's fear of being branded a troublemaker by the park management, Nikki's mouth firmed. No doubt a visit from a medical officer would be seen as snooping. 'That's fine. Pop in any time. I'll ask Grace to fit you in between patients.'

Nikki returned to her desk and buzzed Reception. 'Does Liam have anyone with him, Grace?'

'Last patient left about five minutes ago. Like me to make a cuppa?'

'Not just now, thanks. I'll be with Liam if you need me.'

Liam's dark head shot up when Nikki rapped on his door and swept in. 'Problem?'

'I've just seen another toddler from the caravan park,' she said without preamble. 'I think we have to move very fast, Liam, before we have a full-scale epidemic on our hands. Or a tragedy.'

'Right.' Liam swung to his feet. 'I'd like you with me, please. We'll head straight over to the council offices and report our findings.'

'Don't you mean suspicions?' Nikki countered. 'It's obvious something dodgy is going on at the caravan park.'

'We can't go around making accusations, Nikki.'

'Oh, I can, Liam. Just watch me!'

'Calm down.' His hand fell on her shoulder. 'This is a close community. As the medical officers, we play it by the book, all right?'

Nikki's mouth tightened. 'You mean sit on the fence?'

'I'd call it treading a fine line.' He frowned at her. 'You haven't lost your boots-and-all approach, I see.'

She lifted her chin dismissively and stood back while he opened the door.

'So, who is this council person we have to see?' Nikki asked. It was a few minutes later and they were in Liam's vehicle and heading along the main street.

'Warren Hartley. If anything, he'll be a bit cautious about moving on this.' He added the blunt rider with a warning glance in her direction.

'He'll move,' Nikki asserted with the air of a kitten about to turn into a tiger. 'And if he doesn't, we'll just go to the park ourselves and confront this manager guy.'

'Nik, any investigation will have to go through the proper channels.' Liam brought the Land Rover to a stop outside a low-set red brick building.

Nikki snorted. 'Meanwhile, tiny children are at risk. Surely we can do better than that, Liam?' She turned, her gaze clashing with the dark depths of his.

For a few seconds Liam studied her, then he shook his head, smiling crookedly. 'God, I've missed you.'

Feeling every nerve-end in her body tingle, Nikki contrived to say lightly, 'You could've picked a more opportune moment to tell me.'

'Perhaps I will.' His look was inscrutable. Then, almost absently, placing his hand on her shoulder, Liam leant across her and peered out at the seemingly deserted council offices. 'It's after five. Let's hope they haven't all gone home.'

'Only one way to find out.' Restlessly, she swung out from under the weight of his hand, reaching for the doorhandle.

'Mr Hartley's away on council business for a couple of days,' the receptionist at the information desk informed them. 'Mrs Westermann is standing in for him.'

'Then is she available, please?' Liam stood to his full six feet and placed his hands squarely on the counter. 'It's a matter of urgency.'

Nikki gave him a grateful look. 'A matter of community health,' she emphasised, hoping her statement would add weight to Liam's.

'In that case...' The receptionist picked up the phone.

'We're in luck,' Liam murmured, guiding Nikki

towards a window where they stood for a moment looking out.

'We are?'

'Mmm. Dion Westermann is a former nurse, a very clued-up lady—knows how to get things done.'

'Then, the gods are with us.'

Dion Westermann was in her mid-forties, slender with long fair hair looped into a loose knot at the nape of her neck. 'Liam, hello.' She came out of an office to their left, her smile warm.

'Dion. Good of you to see us.' Liam drew Nikki forward. 'Dr Nicola Barrett, my practice partner.'

'Dr Barrett.' The alderman held out her hand. 'I must say it's very good to have a female practitioner in town.'

'Thank you. And, please, call me Nikki.'

Dion ushered them into her office, waving them into comfortable chairs. 'I understand from Sandra you're concerned about a health issue?'

Briefly but succinctly Liam gave the facts as they knew them.

'So you see, we do really need to sort this before things get out of hand,' Nikki added earnestly.

'Oh, absolutely,' Dion agreed. 'As you probably know, all health matters pertaining to caravan parks come under the council's jurisdiction, so let's see what we can find out, shall we?' She began running information through on her computer screen. 'Ah! According to this, the park is owned by a Kurt Gwatking of Sydney. Perry Phillips is his appointed manager.'

'So...' Nikki exchanged a quick glance with Liam

'…if there's something untoward going on, it's down to this Mr Phillips.'

'Logically, I suppose we could assume that.' The alderman removed her spectacles, leaving them dangling on the keeper-chain around her neck. 'But, then, with the water shortage, perhaps folk are not taking their usual care about personal hygiene and so on.'

'We've thought of all that.' Nikki leaned forward, her expression intense. 'But what if the problem is with the water itself? And my information is that the park has switched the vans over to tank water for domestic use.'

'Well, many people have had no option but to do that,' Dion countered, a small frown pleating her forehead. 'But the council has made sure that our supplier uses only water suitable for human consumption. So, if something's gone wrong with the actual water supply, surely half the townsfolk would be presenting with the symptoms you've described.'

Liam took a deep breath and let it go. 'Although we haven't actually voiced them, I think both Nikki and I have concerns something untoward is going on with the caravan park's own water supply.' He swung to Nikki, his dark brows flicking up in query.

She nodded. 'I think it's a definite possibility,' she said quietly.

'Then say no more.' Dion picked up her phone. 'I'll have one of our people go over there now and take samples for testing. But I'm afraid it'll have to go to Sydney for this new testing regime, immunomagnetic separation, and time-wise that's unfortunate.'

'We could do a very preliminary analysis if that would help,' Nikki offered.

Liam's head spun round, the light from the window illuminating the hard line of his jaw. He gave her a long searching look. 'The slide-under-the-microscope technique?'

Nikki spread her palms in a shrug. 'It may be elementary but it will certainly tell us if there are bugs in the water. We had a scare similar to this when I was in Papua New Guinea.' She felt the need to explain. 'Initially, we did our own very basic sampling so we could act to minimise the risks to people's health.'

'A proper breakdown will have to be left to the lab, of course,' Dion said.

'Naturally. But Liam and I could set the ball rolling.'

The older woman gave a nod of approval. 'That sounds very pro-active. And I thank you very much. I'll get onto it right away. You'll have your sample within the hour.'

'We'll use the facilities in X-Ray,' Liam said. Armed with their water sample, they made their way through the rear entrance of the hospital.

'It's all a bit clandestine, isn't it?' Nikki said grimly.

'Can't be helped. We don't want the dogs barking it before we've something tangible to report.'

'*If* we've something tangible to report.'

Liam's look sharpened. 'You don't doubt it, do you?'

'No…' Nikki gusted a sigh. 'I wish I did.'

It took only seconds to set up their respective microscopes and slides. And only a few seconds more to realise their fears were now realities.

'Good grief…' Liam muttered through his teeth, his gaze narrowing into the microscope lens. 'If this water's ever seen the inside of a filtering plant, I'll walk backwards to Bourke.'

'It's got to be seething with pollutants.' Nikki homed in on her own sample, her voice snapping with anger.

'Breeding lovely bugs like *Cryptosporidium* and *Giardia*,' Liam growled. 'And heaven knows what else.'

Nikki felt sick at the implications. 'This is an appalling situation, Liam. *Giardia* can take months or even years to be eradicated from the system.'

'And this could be just the tip of the iceberg.'

Nikki met his gaze fearfully. 'What about the people who have already left the park and who might have consumed some of the water? We'll have to contact them urgently.'

'We'll have to find them first.' Liam's expression became tight. 'If they're caravanning as such, it's unlikely they'll have left forwarding addresses.'

'We could begin by alerting people through ABC radio.' Nikki brightened. 'Most rural areas can pick up one of their stations, can't they?'

'It's probably the only one they *can* pick up,' Liam affirmed grimly. 'But it's certainly a practical move. The Health Department will have to be notified urgently as well. It'll be up to the Minister to get out a general alert to hospitals and GPs to be on the lookout. But let's not hang about here. Dion is waiting to be informed of our findings.'

'Then do it now, Liam!' Nikki practically pushed him out the door. 'Use the phone in Anna's office. I'll clear up here.'

Liam was just putting the phone down when Nikki caught up with him. 'Feel like a door-knock around the park residents?' He swung to his feet.

'Whatever it takes.'

'Anna can let us have two nurses. Dion will come herself and bring them with her. We'll meet at the park in ten minutes.'

'What about replacement water for the residents?' Nikki asked as they sped outside to the hospital car park.

'The council is organising a load of bottled water to be trucked over there as we speak. They'll have to keep using the bottled stuff until we sort things out.'

'And the park manager?'

'It's out of our hands. Dion has informed the police.' Liam shot out of the parking bay on to the road. 'If the law's been broken, the police are the ones with the authority to lay charges. But, by heck, someone better have answers.'

There was no sign of Dion when they got to the park entrance. Nikki looked at her watch. 'I say we give her another five minutes and if there's still no sign of her, I'm going in.'

'For heaven's sake!' Liam frowned his displeasure. 'You sound like someone from one of those TV police shows. We have to follow protocol, Nikki.'

'Protocol be damned!' Nikki's mouth set determinedly. 'Another toddler could be drinking this foul water as we speak! I'm a doctor. Surely, I have the authority to approach the park manager on a health matter?'

For a moment they looked at each other and Liam swore under his breath.

The seconds ticked slowly by. 'There must have been some last-minute hitch,' Liam growled. 'These things happen. They'll be here directly.'

'I'm not waiting any longer, Liam.' Nikki flung open her door on the passenger side. 'Don't try to stop me!' She shrugged off his hand as he tried to delay her. 'Look...' She softened slightly. 'I'll remember I'm a doctor first, if that's what you're worried about.'

'We don't know what kind of character this Perry Phillips is,' Liam pointed out, his narrowed gaze going beyond the gates to the demountable building that was obviously the office.

Nikki made a face. 'Do you think he might have a gun?'

'Don't even go there, Nikki—even in jest.' Liam ploughed a hand through his hair in obvious frustration. 'Look, one of us should stay here and wait for Dion, otherwise the whole exercise will be in disarray from the start. You stay and *I'll* front Mr Phillips.'

'No!' Nikki shook her head. 'You're the community health officer, you should be here to accompany Dion and her party. But I think, as a matter of urgency, one of us should be in there now, speaking to the parents of the children we've treated.'

'All right.' Liam's shoulders slumped as if he had no choice. 'I can see your point. But the first whiff of trouble, Nikki, you're out of there. Understood?'

'Yes, Liam,' she said with mock meekness. 'I'll need the names of your two families, please.'

'Jansen and Meier.' The names came out on a sigh.

She nodded in satisfaction. 'Now, I just have to get the relevant site numbers from Mr Phillips. I think I'll take my bag,' she added, swinging out of the Land Rover. 'That way, my visit will appear authentic.'

'Don't rock any boats,' Liam warned tensely, alighting from his side of the vehicle. 'You have your mobile?'

Nikki looked skywards briefly. 'Yes, Liam.'

'Keep it switched on.' He leant abruptly and took her face between his hands. 'I hate throwing you to the lions like this, Nik.'

She lifted her hand and placed it over one of his. 'I can take care of myself, Liam. I've had to for a long time now.'

And why didn't that statement make him feel one jot happier? He gave an odd little shrug and let her go.

Nikki was barely through the entrance gates when she decided the place was already giving her the creeps. Darkness had fallen quickly, as though someone had thrown a cloak over the sun, and the lighting was poor at best.

Beating back a shadowy unease, she mounted the

shallow steps to the demountable. There was a faint
light visible through one of the wire-meshed windows and another on the narrow landing. She took a
deep breath and raising her hand, rapped as loudly
as she dared on the door marked OFFICE.

It took an age for the door to be opened.

'Yeah?' A bulky man narrowed his piggy eyes at
Nikki.

'Mr Phillips?' Nikki swallowed, a prickle of alarm
teasing the back of her neck.

'Who wants to know?' The smell of alcohol curled
off the man's breath in nauseating waves.

Nikki reeled back. 'I'm…Dr Barrett from the surgery. The children of several of the residents have
been poorly. I've come to check them over. I'd like
the van site numbers of Bycroft, Jansen and Meiers,
please.'

Perry Phillips folded his arms, blocking the doorway. 'Don't want no doctors snooping round here.
Now, clear out!'

Nikki put her medical case down and straightened
to her full five feet four, grabbing her courage in both
hands. 'What's your problem, Mr Phillips? I've
asked you civilly for directions to three of your park
residents. I expect you to give them to me.'

'Or what?' Perry Phillips thrust his unshaven face
in front of her.

Nikki felt her hands curl into fists, everything in
her wanting to thump his fat belly until he gave her
the information she needed. Instead, she thought of
Liam's warning and took a steadying breath. She
brought her chin up. 'You might intimidate the fe-

male residents, *Mr* Phillips, but you don't frighten me. Now, give me the information.'

'Or what?' His tone thickened menacingly.

'Or I'll call the police!' Nikki threw caution to the winds and pushed past the man into the office.

'You'll call nobody, you flamin' busybody! Hear me?' He lifted a fist threateningly. 'Now, get outa here!'

Nikki felt a jarring crunch and gave a cry of pain as the manager's beefy hands caught her by the shoulders. Her slight body was no match for his brute strength, and she was yanked roughly through the door and shoved backwards onto the outside landing. She gave a gasp, feeling herself falling, falling—and then caught. Hard.

In a haze of terror she realised that whatever had stopped her fall had human form. Dear heaven—did Phillips have reinforcements?

Fear whimpered out of her throat, ending in a choking sob.

'I've got you, Nik... I've got you...'

The words echoed and spun through her head, then she was turned into protective arms and held. Oh, Liam. Oh, thank God.

'I miscalculated badly, didn't I?' Nikki was sitting huddled in her dressing-gown at the kitchen table, a small Scotch in front of her.

Hands rammed into his back pockets, Liam paced the floor. 'I think I lost ten years off my life when I saw that cretin trying to shove you down the steps. Hell, Nikki! Don't ever do anything like that again!'

'All right.' She held up her hands for mercy. 'I've learned my lesson. Can we drop it now?'

Liam dragged out a chair and sat opposite her. 'Phillips is in police custody now at any rate. He'll be charged with assault for starters.'

'And they'll pin the dodgy water rap on him for sure.' Nikki was fast regaining her equilibrium. She took a mouthful of her drink. 'Did Dion say what delayed her?'

'A chapter of stupid mishaps.' Liam frowned into his drink. 'First her car tyre was flat and all the council vehicles were locked away for the night. So she ran back inside the building to ring for a taxi. On the way she fell up the steps, which kind of slowed her down. Then there were no taxis available…'

'Oh, lord.' Nikki gave a strangled laugh. 'It would be funny if it weren't so serious.' She looked over the rim of her glass at Liam. 'At least everyone at the park has been notified now and been supplied with their bottled water. So could we say all's well that ends well?'

Liam smiled a little crookedly. 'Except for Dion's skinned knees and you being frightened half to death—I suppose we could.'

CHAPTER SIX

'IS IT very difficult working with Liam when you're not married any more?'

Nikki pondered Grace's blunt question for a few seconds. It was two weeks later. Liam was off on one of his outlying patients' clinics and the women were enjoying a coffee-break during a lull in the afternoon surgery. 'I'm loving it really,' she said, surprised by her answer.

'And it's not making life, well, a bit complicated?'

'We've been so busy.' Nikki lifted a shoulder dismissively. 'And at night we're so dog-tired we just fall into bed. Into separate beds,' she qualified, giving a ripple of embarrassed laughter.

Grace tapped her thumbnail absently against the handle of her coffee-mug. 'Everyone thinks very highly of you.'

'Better let Liam know, then,' Nikki joked, unbelievably warmed by the other's words. 'He might decide to let me stay on.'

'Surely there's no question of that?'

'We agreed on a three-month contract.' Nikki threw caution to the winds, letting her tongue run away with the confidential information. But she was feeling slightly desperate. Every day was a day nearer to the end of her agreed time in Wirilda. And since that searing kiss when they'd finished planting the herb garden, Liam had been steadfastly keeping his distance.

Nikki was being eaten up with indecision, her heart bouncing sickeningly each time they so much as brushed against each other in the normal course of sharing a house.

And suddenly she feared it was all happening again, the absolute need she felt around him to be held, comforted.

Loved.

But did Liam feel any of that? Or would he be glad to see the back of her at the end of her three-month tenure?

Seeing the sudden little droop to the younger woman's mouth, Grace skilfully changed conversational lanes. 'Perry Phillips finally admitted to importing inferior water for the tanks. Did you hear?'

Nikki clicked her tongue. 'My patients were full of it this morning. Naturally he didn't have a leg to stand on once the lab results came back. Fancy thinking he could get away with it, though.'

'And charging the residents almost double for the privilege. The hide of the man! I believe the owner was completely in the dark about his goings-on. He's taken over managing the park himself until he can employ someone trustworthy.'

Nikki's gaze sharpened. 'You mean there's a job going there?'

'Well, I imagine so.' Grace rose to her feet and began gathering up their mugs. 'Did you have someone in mind?'

'Perhaps…' Nikki lifted her gaze, catching the shimmer of mid-afternoon sunlight through the lacy fretwork of the pepper trees outside the window. 'I need to make a quick phone call, Grace.' Decisively, she swung upright and pushed her chair in. 'Stall my next patient for a few minutes, will you, please?'

Nikki's last patient for the day was Sonia Reed. 'We're just passing through,' the young woman said a bit awkwardly. 'My family owns a small circus.'

Nikki smiled. 'What an interesting lifestyle.'

'Most of the time.' Sonia's blue eyes clouded momentarily. 'But I have a three-year-old now and it does get a bit hectic trying to keep her amused while we're on the road.'

'I'm sure it does.' Nikki waited, realising it was going to take time for Sonia Reed to get to the reason for her visit.

'The thing is, Dr Barrett...' Nervously, Sonia interlinked her fingers and held them against her chest. 'I, uh, was at the local laundrette yesterday and I got talking to a couple of other mums there...'

'As you do,' Nikki came in with a twinkle.

Sonia nodded. 'We got talking about our kids. And about their health.' She swallowed and then said with a rush, 'They said you were very tuned in to your patients.'

'Well, thank you for the compliment.' Nikki gave a slight smile. 'So, is there something I can help you with today?'

'It's my daughter—Emily.' Sonia met Nikki's gaze uncertainly. 'She's been diagnosed with atopic eczema. She was prescribed a steroid cream.'

'And was there a problem with that?' Nikki

wanted to know. It was the standard treatment after all.

'It doesn't seem to be getting any better and I wondered if there was anything new on the market I could try.'

Nikki stifled a sigh. She didn't like diagnosing off the cuff like this. 'Was there a reason you didn't bring Emily with you today?'

Sonia looked uncomfortable. 'I…just thought I'd ask while we were here in Wirilda. Em's been so scratchy and irritable with the rash. She finally dropped off to sleep so I just thought while I had a spare minute I'd come in and ask. It'll be ages before we get back to one of the big towns again.'

Nikki sensed the young mother's anguish, sympathising with her dilemma. It must be disconcerting to be forever on the move with no family doctor nearby, no place to really call home. 'Well, as far as atopic eczema is concerned, its presence is usually related to allergies,' she said carefully. 'Diet also plays a part. So it follows that any food that may be aggravating Emily's condition should be avoided. Did you see a dietitian somewhere along the line?'

Sonia shook her head. 'It was just a little rural hospital where I took her initially. The doctor did suggest I see someone when I got back to the city…'

Nikki's gaze widened in query. 'When do you leave Wirilda?'

'Probably midmorning tomorrow. We've a show tonight.'

'Could you pop Emily in to see me before you leave, do you think? I'll check her over and make sure there's nothing else beside the eczema worrying her.'

'Yes, I can do that.' Sonia leaned forward earnestly. 'And you mentioned diet, Dr Barrett. Is there something I could be doing to help her? Anything?'

'Well, you could certainly note if there are any foods that seem to make Emily's eczema worse.' Nikki pulled her pad towards her and began writing. 'The culprits are sometimes milk, wheat and maybe orange juice. If there is a likely suspect, avoid it for a week or two and see if Emily's condition improves.'

'That sounds simple enough.'

'It is, Sonia, but this is where the advice of a dietitian is essential. If you take Emily off one food, you should be supplementing it with another more suitable one. If you don't, she could become deficient in some nutrient by avoiding that food. Does that make sense?'

Sonia bit her lips together and nodded. 'Maybe it's time Marcus and I left the circus and settled somewhere…'

And that was one minefield she had no intention of accompanying her patient through, Nikki thought grimly. Lord knew, she had enough of her own lying in wait. Instead, she tried to lighten the atmosphere.

'There are a few old-fashioned methods that still work for eczema, you know. For instance, getting rid of the soap often helps. Instead, use an oat sock.'

'Sorry?' Sonia blinked.

Nikki grinned. 'It's very simple. Just cut off the foot from an old pair of your tights and fill it with a couple of handfuls of rolled oats. Use it instead of soap when you bathe Emily.'

'And that'll help?'

'It's very good for the skin in general. Much more economical too.' Nikki got to her feet, signalling the consultation was at an end. There was nothing more she cared to add until she'd examined the child. 'Make an appointment for tomorrow with Grace as you leave.' She smiled encouragingly. 'I'll check Emily over and we'll go from there.'

Liam drove back into the town centre. It was late and he was tired. All the way home his thoughts had been pulling him every which way.

He wondered what kind of day Nikki had had. Had there been any emergencies? Would she have coped? His mouth tightened. Silly question. Her coping skills these days continued to amaze him.

And intimidate him.

When she'd first arrived in Wirilda, he'd entertained vague thoughts she might have needed him. In his innermost heart he admitted he'd wanted her to. But, within the practice at least, she'd proved beyond any shadow of doubt that those days were gone. Nikki Barrett was her own person. And it appeared that was how she preferred it.

'Oh, hell!'

He called in briefly at the surgery in case there was anything needing his attention. Apart from a few e-mails Grace had printed out and left for him, there was nothing urgent.

Unloading the patient files he'd taken with him for his outlying clinic, he made a cursory security check throughout the building. Everything was spot on. He blew out a short sigh and turned, making his way out through the front door to the car port.

Nikki's nerves were shredding. She'd heard the sub-dued phut-phut of the Land Rover as Liam had come up the drive and slid into the carport.

He was home at last.

The reality sent her heart swooping like a drunken butterfly, the sweet sting of anticipation slithering up her spine. Agitatedly, she touched a hand to the silky fabric of her skirt, wondering belatedly whether she'd gone over the top.

But this evening, for reasons she couldn't even begin to fathom, she'd wanted to look special for Liam. Instead of her usual shorts and T-shirt, she'd pulled out one of the only two dresses she'd brought with her, slipping it on quickly before she could change her mind.

What she'd chosen was a new-look summer cre-ation she'd bought at the Coast. The top, what there was of it, was held up with tiny shoestring straps while the frilly hemline of the skirt bounced sexily around her calves.

Looking in the mirror, she'd decided she loved the saffron colour, its vibrancy showing off her tanned complexion. And just wearing such a dress made her feel cool and feminine—and something else. Desirable?

Almost mechanically, Liam hitched up his medical case from the passenger seat and swung out of the

Land Rover, wishing he could slough off the dismal mood that seemed to have settled on him.

Making his way through the courtyard, he brought his head up sharply, sniffing the air. Something smelt good and the aroma was coming from the kitchen.

Suddenly he felt a lightness in his step, a twist of excitement ambushing him out of nowhere. At the top of the steps he paused and looked around him. His jaw dropped.

This had to be Nikki's doing.

The wooden outdoor table was set elegantly for dinner, white cloth, cutlery and glasses sparkling in the subdued lamplight, the scent of a potted jasmine lending an almost sensual pleasure to the atmosphere.

He stared past the cacti in their bright pots to the tall candles waiting to be lit. And drew in a sharp breath. Just what kind of statement was his former wife making? What kind of response did she want from him? Strands of emotion unravelled, knotting his gut, intermingling with the oddest kind of pain he couldn't account for.

Oh, damn. Blinking, he turned up his head and the ceiling blurred and momentarily went out of focus. Double damn. So many dreams lost. So much of their lives thrown away…

He blew out a huge controlling breath and squared his shoulders. He couldn't stand here all night. Swallowing convulsively, he made his way slowly across the deck towards the kitchen.

'Nikki?'

'In here.' Nikki's throat was so dry she could hardly speak.

'Hi…' Liam slid his case into a corner and then

straightened, his heart beating so heavily he could feel it thundering inside his chest. 'Are we having a party?'

Nikki shook her head, the action sending highlights bouncing off her short little bob. 'You've had such a long day…' She paused and licked her lips. 'I thought you deserved a treat.'

'Looking at you is quite a treat in itself.' His gaze flickered all the way down her body and back again. 'You look stunning, Nik…'

'It's the dress.' She blushed, her hand flying to her chest to cover the peep of cleavage. 'Uh, glass of wine or would you like a shower first?'

'A shower, I think.' His mouth curled ruefully. 'I'd kill for a nice long soak.'

'Wishful thinking, Doctor. I've done lamb with rosemary for dinner,' she tacked on breathlessly.

'*Our* rosemary?' His smile was teasing.

'Of course.' Something boiled over on the stove and with a little gasp she turned to rescue it, her concentration shot to pieces.

'Did you burn yourself?' Liam was right behind her.

'I'm fine.' She flapped her fingers for a second, before quickly turning the heat down.

'Show me.' His hand reached out to circle her wrist.

'Liam, it's fine,' she protested on a laugh.

'Let me fix it,' he countered softly. Lifting her hand, he pressed an achingly slow kiss to the tender underside of her wrist. 'There you are. All better…'

Nikki took a shallow breath. Suddenly, inexplicably, the atmosphere was charged with danger like the hidden undertow of a giant wave. She made a tiny sound in her throat. Her eyes, wide and slightly startled, met his and her lips parted a fraction.

It was too much for Liam. His throat worked as he rasped her name, drawing her into his arms and lowering his mouth to hers.

Her lips tasted like nectar, so soft, so giving, parting to allow him access. He heard her whimper as she signalled her need, sliding her arms around his waist and urging him closer.

A convulsive shiver ran through him. The slow-burning heat he'd struggled to contain for the past weeks raged out of control, the feel of her ripe, warm body pressed against him almost sending him over the edge. All the suppressed passion of the past six years rose up, demanding release.

Nikki. He wanted her, needed her in a way he'd forgotten he could need, and only the dark reminder that she was no longer his wife stopped him from scooping her up and taking her through to the wide double bed.

On a sharp indrawn breath he pulled back, staring down into the liquid depths of her eyes. They were glistening pools of desire. Wanting him.

'Wow…' Nikki took a little jagged breath, just resisting the compulsion to slide her hand down the opening of his shirt and feel the contours of his chest with her palm. She stepped back, a residual heat shooting through her leaving her weak and trembling. 'You OK…?'

He looked at her through half-closed eyes. 'No.'

'Um…perhaps a shower will help,' she said softly, her voice gliding like silk over his nerve ends.

His dark head on an angle, he looked broodingly at her. 'Perhaps I'd better make it a cold one.'

Liam came out on the deck a little later, showered and dressed in jeans and a soft white shirt.

'Feeling better?' Nikki looked up from lighting the last of the candles. 'Oh, lord.' Her laugh was fractured, nerves gripping her insides like tentacles. 'I sound like your doctor.'

'You are my doctor.'

She swallowed drily. Even in the subdued light she could feel the intensity of his gaze. 'We're just about ready.'

'Like me to open the wine?'

She lifted a hand and held it to her throat. 'Ah…yes, if you wouldn't mind. And carve the roast?'

His eyes swept her from head to toe. 'My pleasure.'

'This is fantastic, Nik.' Liam complimented her, as the dessert's tangy Jaffa flavour slid over his tongue.

Nikki shrugged. 'These days I enjoy preparing food.' She didn't add there was something very sensual about preparing food for one's lover. Except Liam wasn't her lover. Not now. Perhaps he never would be again.

'What happened to us, Nik?' As if he'd read her thoughts, Liam slowly drew his gaze from his now-empty dessert glass to her.

Nikki took refuge in flippancy. 'We stuffed up, Liam. Big time.' With fingers that shook she crushed her serviette and dropped it beside her plate. 'Cup of tea?'

He ignored her question. Instead, he reached out and stilled her hand. 'We could have had a child by now…' His thumb began smoothing gently over her knuckles. 'A sassy little girl like her mother. I look at you and still want you like crazy, Nik.'

Her throat lumped. 'Yes, well…'

'I think I get to you too,' he murmured. 'And it's not the same. It's better. So much better.'

'Liam…' She swallowed again, harder. His thumb was sending shivers through her arm.

'Do you want me, Nikki?'

A quiet desperation settled over her. She pulled her hand away. 'I never did get over you. No one else has ever made me feel the way you do—did.'

'Have you had many lovers?'

Her heart kicked and she swallowed. 'Don't ask those kinds of question, Liam. I'm not answering them. Once the divorce was made absolute, to all intents and purposes we were single again. Anyway, I've been too busy working to have any time for lovers.'

His fist clenched on the tablecloth. 'I almost got engaged once.'

'You did?' Nikki was alarmed at the stab of jealousy she felt. 'What happened?'

He jerked a shoulder self-deprecatingly. 'We were both carrying baggage. What we had was a kind of clutching-at-straws scenario. Thank heaven, we woke up and decided to end it. It was pretty soon after that I came to Wirilda.'

In the short silence that followed, Nikki's thoughts

flew back to when she and Liam had first met. Pictures flashed quickly, randomly through her mind. The way he'd kept glancing at her when they'd sat across from each other at one of the long tables in the university library.

And he'd cleared his throat and asked her opinion about something. And she'd given it and he'd listened as if every word she'd uttered had been edged with gold. And when, finally, they'd left the library and gone for a coffee together, she'd felt as though she'd known him for ever. But how wrong she'd been. As later events had proved, she hadn't really known him at all...

'So...why did you really come to Wirilda, Nikki?'

She swooped back to the present with a ragged sigh. Why had she come? She hardly knew any more. 'It was a spur-of-the-moment thing. After MSF, my skills were hardly being stretched in a state-of-the-art city practice.'

'I could have been married again.' His eyes never left her face. 'Would you have still wanted to come?'

'I knew you weren't.'

He looked taken aback. And then his dark brows kicked together in a frown. 'I suppose you had your father check me out.'

Her heart twisted painfully. 'My father has no influence over my life these days.'

He laughed shortly. 'Until it suits him.'

'Just leave my father out of this!' Nikki felt her nerve-ends stretching to their fragile limits. 'If you must know, I've kept in touch with Clare. She told me.'

'My mother?' he rasped. 'Good grief!' He rocked

back in his chair and thrust his gaze up towards the ceiling.

'We've always got on together,' Nikki justified, picking up her serviette again and twisting it through her fingers. A tiny smile activated the dimple in her cheek. 'Clare still sends me a card on my birthday.'

'The two of you.' Liam sounded as though he still couldn't believe it. 'In cahoots.'

Nikki gave an impatient little tsk. 'You're acting as though there's something odd about keeping in touch. Clare and I were once related by marriage.'

Liam scrubbed lean fingers across his cheekbones. 'I'm well aware of that. Do you want to be again?' he tacked on softly. 'Is that why you came to Wirilda, Nikki? To give us another shot at being married?'

'I…' She bit down on her bottom lip. 'I did really want to help you in the practice. And…I thought perhaps if we got to know each other again…' She found her eyes drawn helplessly to his.

'I'd never let you walk away a second time, Nikki.'

'You were the one who walked,' she pointed out, her voice raw with emotion.

'Semantics.' He rocked his hand dismissively and a bleak kind of silence settled over them.

When the phone rang, it took several seconds for either of them to register the fact. Then they both went to move but Liam got to his feet first. 'I'll get it.'

'You just want to stick me with the washing-up.' Nikki tried for lightness, somehow grateful for the interruption.

'That was Brett Gilroy.' Liam strode back into the kitchen a little later, his expression serious.

'The sergeant?' Nikki placed the tray of washing-up on the sink.

'What's up?'

'Couple of tourists in strife—well, one is. He's fallen down a disused well. His mate walked about five kilometres back to get help.'

'For heaven's sake!' Nikki glanced at her watch. 'When did all this happen?'

'Some time this afternoon, it seems.'

She gazed at Liam in disbelief. 'Didn't they have a mobile?'

'Apparently not.'

'When will tourists realise the vastness of this country?' Nikki snapped her disapproval. 'Some of them are totally ill-prepared for emergencies. They wander off as though they're going for a stroll through the Botanic Gardens!'

'Yes, well, we've seen a few of those,' Liam agreed bluntly. 'But let's give this young guy A for effort. He took off to get help but became disorientated so he waited until nightfall, hoping there'd be some lights somewhere to guide him. He finally made it to a farmhouse—the Simpsons', actually. Danny rang the police.'

'We'd better get out there, then.' Nikki's professional instincts flew into overdrive.

He frowned. 'You don't *have* to, Nikki. I'll manage.'

'I'm coming with you, Liam.'

'OK.' He spread his hands in compliance. 'I'm not

about to knock back another pair of experienced hands.'

'Good.' Nikki swept a teatowel off the rack and covered the tray of dirty dishes. 'Just give me a couple of minutes to change out of my party gear.'

'Pity…' Leaning over, he brushed her lips with his. 'Will you wear it for me again?' he asked softly. 'Soon?'

She hesitated just a second, then with a slight shake of her head she turned and tore down the hallway to her bedroom.

So what did that little shake mean? Perhaps? Get real? Get lost? Liam swung his medical case up on to the table, snapping open the locks to check its contents. His mouth pulled tight. Why had he done all that grandstanding six years ago and walked out on their marriage?

Fool.

He felt a huge lump form in his throat and swallowed convulsively. He wanted his wife back in his bed, real and warmly giving. Not just the memory of her lips and the way her body called to his, taunting him through the lonely nights…

Armed with a trauma kit from the hospital, they travelled in Liam's Land Rover. 'The arrangement is we meet at the Simpsons' and go from there.' Liam gunned the motor along the straight stretch of country road.

'So, apart from the ambulance, who's in on this jaunt?' Nikki wanted to know.

'Brett, of course. He heads up the local state emergency team. Their vehicle with the rescue gear is kept at the police station, which is a plus. But he'll have to try and get a team together, which could be difficult. Danny's a member so he'll be an asset. He's lived here all his life. Let's hope he'll have a fair idea where this old well is located.'

'Do we have any idea what injuries our patient has?'

'We'll have to wait and see, I guess.' Liam placed his hand on her jeans-clad thigh and squeezed. 'Good to have you along, Nik.'

'Sure.' She inhaled deeply, recognising the flutter of uncertainty in her stomach. Despite her experience with MSF, delivering medicine on the trot like this still unnerved her. 'How does one fall into a well in broad daylight, though, Liam?'

He grunted. 'Easier than you might think. Obviously it hasn't been used for years so back when it was decided to close it, some attempt would have been made to cover it over.'

'How?' She glanced at him sharply. 'With logs and things?'

'Mmm. And with time they'll have become overgrown with weeds and stuff, which will have only served to camouflage the rotting wood beneath. And there you have an accident waiting to happen.'

Nikki gnawed gently on her bottom lip. 'I, um, guess the hole will be fairly deep.'

'Yep.'

'And are we looking at a biggish area?'

Liam lifted a shoulder. 'Six by six perhaps, in the old measurement.'

'The size of a small room,' she considered. 'That will at least give us space to work on our patient.'

'Maybe,' Liam sounded sceptical. 'More likely there'll be rubble at the base of it. And I mean anything from rocks to old furniture. Usually some effort is extended to part-fill the hole to make it less of a hazard before it's covered over. Small animals can find their way in as well. Rats, especially.'

Charming. Nikki suppressed a shudder. She only hoped they were dead ones, their remains long gone.

'Here's the entry to the Simpsons' place now.' Liam swung the Land Rover through the farm gates, the big tyres rattling over the metal grid. 'Farmhouse up there on the hill.'

Nikki peered out at the pinprick of light. For the uninitiated there was no place as lonely as the bush at night, she thought grimly. And for the man trapped down the well it must be doubly frightening.

CHAPTER SEVEN

'THIS is Joel.' Brett Gilroy cast a swift glance at the faces assembled around the Simpson's kitchen table. 'The young fella who's come to get help for his mate.'

'Thanks, everyone, for turning out—' Joel scooped a hand through his long fair hair. 'Nathan and I are archaeology students. We'd heard of some good finds hereabouts. We left our car and went off on a reccy. Didn't realise we'd got so far off course. We were still trying to decide which way to go when Nate fell down the hole.'

Nikki tilted her head towards the student. 'Do you know if he's injured?'

'He made a hell of a racket when he fell in.' Joel's throat worked as he swallowed uncomfortably. 'I yelled out to him. He kind of groaned and then…then there was nothing.' He turned anguished eyes on the gathering. 'I took off to get help.'

'Was he carrying water?' Liam asked.

'He had a backpack.'

Liam's mouth drew in. If the youngster had been caught on something or injured, he might not have been able to access it. Well, they'd worry about that when they got there.

Brett cleared his throat. 'Unfortunately, I wasn't able to gather up a full team. The two guys I was

depending on were at the pub and no use for anything,' he lamented.

'Probably would've ended up in the hole as well.'
Danny Simpson gave a laconic grin. 'What about
Roz and Janice?'

The sergeant looked at Nikki. 'They're our only
two women volunteers but they can't leave their kids
at night while their menfolk are working away from
home.'

'Sign of the times, I guess.' Baz Inall chimed in
for the first time. 'I'm on my own in the ambulance
as well. Couldn't rustle up a partner.'

Nikki wanted to scream. While they sat about
chatting, there was a man lying injured somewhere.
She opened her mouth and snapped it shut at the
warning press of Liam's thigh against hers under the
table. Leave it to me, his direct look clearly said,
before he turned to Danny Simpson. 'So, mate, you
have a fair idea of the location of the well?'

'Yep, no worries, Doc. I'll go with Brett in the
SES truck. The rest of you follow, OK? Oh, Michelle
left a couple of Thermos flasks and some sandwiches
for us before she went to work. I'll bring those along.
We could be a while.'

'Right, everyone,' Brett launched himself upright.
'Let's go! Ah, Baz, would you mind taking Joel with
you?'

The whole meeting had taken only a few minutes
but to Nikki it had felt more like hours. 'I'm sure
rockets have been launched in less time,' she fumed
to Liam as they climbed back into the Land Rover.

'Settle down, Nikki.' Liam stated the engine and
fell into convoy behind the ambulance. 'These guys

don't react with the speed of a casualty department but every move they make is calculated and with very good reason. At an accident scene they have to take everyone's safety on board. Personally, I'd trust any one of them with my life.'

'Point taken.' Nikki sighed and sank back against the headrest. 'I just want to get there and get the job done, that's all.'

'And we will,' Liam pointed out. 'But rushing in like a bull at a gate and possibly getting injured ourselves isn't going to help our patient, is it?'

'No.'

The truth of Liam's statement was borne out. And much more swiftly than Nikki could have imagined.

Danny had led them unerringly to the site of the old well, and within minutes he and Brett had erected a tripod arrangement over the top and positioned high-powered torches to aid the rescue.

'OK, who's going down?' Brett held out the sturdy safety belt, his question tracking between the two medics.

'We'll both go,' Liam said brusquely. 'Do you have another belt, Brett?'

The sergeant dug into his box of gear. 'Got a dozen of 'em,' he replied calmly.

'Right, Nikki.' Liam swung the trauma pack onto his back. 'Let's do it, shall we?'

Nikki's heart quickened. The gaping hole where Nathan had plunged through looked like an indistinct grey shadow. And very uninviting. 'I take it we're hooked up to this pulley thing and get lowered in.'

'That's right.' Liam seemed to be taking all the

time in the world to reassure her. 'I'll drop in first and the guys will retrieve the rope and send you down. And after we've done all we can for our patient, we'll yell for Baz to be lowered with the retrieval stretcher. Understood?'

'Fine…'

It seemed only seconds later that she found herself swinging down, giving a little gasp as she landed unevenly on a pile of rocks. Unhooking herself from the guide rope, she wrapped her arms around her midriff and took in a controlling breath. There was certainly an odour in the cavity but nothing she couldn't handle. Raising her head, she called, 'Liam?'

'Over here.' Liam was several metres away, holding a torch, the powerful light illuminating their patient.

'What do we have?' Nikki picked her way carefully towards him.

'Don't know yet. But it looks like he's coming round. It's OK, Nathan.' Liam's manner was calmly reassuring. 'I'm Liam and this is Nikki. We're doctors.'

The youngster sucked air in through trembling lips. 'Thought I was a gonner. Leg…' he groaned. 'Pain's awesome.'

Nikki felt her heart lurch, seeing the irregularity of the lad's left leg. From the position in which he was lying it was obvious he'd struck a boulder jutting from the side of the well as he'd fallen. The pain he must be in. She looked a question at Liam. 'Fractured neck of femur?'

'Looks like it. Take it easy now, son.' Liam gently lifted Nathan's head and applied the oxygen mask.

'I'll check his breath sounds.' Nikki slid open a section of the medical kit and took out a stethoscope. She flicked it over Nathan's chest. 'Not too bad,' she murmured, laying the stethoscope aside. Then, carefully, she began palpating his stomach.

Liam nodded in approval. They both knew the possibility of internal bleeding could not be ignored. 'I'll get a line in,' he said whipping a tourniquet around Nathan's arm. 'Blood's a bit slow…' He began tapping urgently to prompt a vein to the surface. 'OK—I've got it.' He slid a cannula into the vein.

'He needs pain relief, urgently.' Nikki kept a watchful eye on their patient. 'But I'd prefer to under-prescribe. He's a rather slight build.'

'Let's go with morphine, five milligrams, and ten of Maxolon. We don't want him throwing up everywhere. We'll follow with fifty of pethidine. That should get him through transportation to the hospital.'

Nikki began preparing the painkiller and antiemetic. 'Are you allergic to anything you know of, Nathan?'

Eyes dulled with pain, the young man shook his head.

'Hang in there, mate.' Liam touched his hand to Nathan's dark crewcut. He glanced at Nikki. 'Ready?'

She nodded, quickly swabbing the cannula and shooting the first two drugs home, praying the injection would work—and soon.

'Right.' Liam's voice was clipped. 'Let's start

splinting. The sooner we get him out of here the better.'

'His breathing's easier.' Nikki watched Liam place the supportive splints between the young man's legs. 'Bandages now?'

'Nice thick ones.'

'So, we send him out by CareFlight, do we?' Nikki surmised, working quickly to bind Nathan's injured leg to his good one.

'They've been alerted.' Liam glanced at his watch. 'Our ambulance will meet them at the airstrip. It's a clear night for flying. They shouldn't have a problem. We'll send him to the Royal.' He looked down at Nathan's still form. 'I should think you could administer that shot of pethidine now, Nikki. I'm just going to give the guys a shout. We're ready for the stretcher.'

'OK.' As Liam moved away from her peripheral vision, Nikki felt the cave-like atmosphere close in on her. She listened, fixing on each tiny sound, suppressing a shudder as a piece of debris, insignificant in size, hissed eerily as it fell and then faded into silence.

Oh, lord… She had to get herself together. She had a job to do. Give Nathan the drug. About to draw up the dose, she stopped and froze. Something was wrong here.

Dreadfully wrong.

'Li-am!' Her anguished cry echoed off the earthen walls.

Nathan was gulping, his eyes rolling back in his head, his colour a ghastly grey. Nikki made a little sound of distress in her throat. If she didn't act, they'd have a tragedy on their hands. In one swift movement she ripped Nathan's shirt open and began chest compressions.

Liam's shadow fell beside her. 'What's happened?' he barked.

'He's throwing a PE!'

Liam's expletive scorched the air. A pulmonary embolism. He grabbed for the lifesaving equipment. He would have to intubate. Damn it to hell. Where was second sight when you needed it? All the components for a PE were there. A serious fracture. Fat escaping from the break gumming up the arteries. Damn, damn and double damn!

Liam's jaw was clamped tight. Skilfully, he passed the tube down Nathan's trachea, attaching it to the oxygen. 'Breathe!' he grated. 'Come on!'

With mounting dread, Nikki swung her gaze and watched Liam check and recheck the carotid pulse in Nathan's neck. He shook his head.

'Time's running out. We'll have to zap him. I'll get the life-pack. We're not losing him, Nikki.' Liam's voice roughened. 'I'm counting on you.'

Nikki's face was intense. Every compression meant life for Nathan. Her heart began to pound against her ribs, her pulse thumping in her wrists and throat. She began feeling light-headed, perspiration patching wetly across her forehead and in the small of her back. 'Liam, hurry…' She found herself trying to breathe for the boy.

'This is a bloody nightmare.' Liam got into position. 'Be ready to take over the bag when I defibrillate,' he snapped.

Nikki found added strength from somewhere. Nathan's life could depend on their teamwork now.

'OK, do it!'

Almost in slow motion she reached out and took over the Air Viva bag.

'And clear!'

Nikki dropped the bag and spun back, praying the volts of electricity would do their work and kick-start the heart's rhythm.

'Zilch…' Liam hissed the word between clenched teeth. 'Let's go to two hundred. Clear!'

Nikki strove to keep her panic at bay, aware only of its grip in her abdomen and the slow slide of sweat between her breasts. She swung her gaze to the monitor. The trace was still flat.

'Start compressions again, Nikki.' Liam looked haunted. 'I'm giving him adrenalin.'

Nikki gasped, 'We're running out of options.'

Liam's mouth clenched into a thin line. His fingers curled around the mini-jet, already prepared with the lifesaving drug. 'Come on, baby—work!' he implored, sending the long needle neatly between Nathan's ribs and into his heart.

'Clear!' He activated the charge and their combined gazes swivelled to the monitor. The trace bleeped and then staggered into a rhythm. 'Yes!' Liam roared. 'We've done it, Nik! You beauty!'

'Oh…' Nikki felt tears of reaction coursing down her cheeks. Hastily, she blinked them away, holding the heels of her hands against her eyes, gathering her composure.

'Hey, Nik.' Liam's arm came round her shoulders,

hugging her. 'Lighten up, hmm? We've got him back.'

'Oh, thank God...' she said huskily, turning her face into his shoulder.

'He's waking up.' Liam gave her a little shake. 'Look!'

Their patient was indeed waking up, fear and confusion clouding his eyes.

'It's OK, Nate.' Nikki beat back the last of the tears and swallowed. 'You'll be fine.' She took his hand and squeezed. 'We've managed a small miracle.'

'Right.' Liam cleared the lump from his throat. 'Think a shot of midazolam is called for here?'

'Yes.' Nikki drew in a deep breath. She felt hollowed out. 'Would you do it, please?' The drug would act as a light anaesthetic and ease Nathan over the trauma of the next couple of hours. Added to that, its amnesic properties would help to stave off post-traumatic shock.

Baz loomed out of the shadow, towing the collapsible stretcher. 'Nice work, folks,' he said quietly. 'Could have been a whole different story, couldn't it?'

Nikki felt as though she'd been to hell and back.

Swallowing hard on the tightness in her throat, she pulled herself upright. 'He's ready to move now, Baz. We've got him back in sinus rhythm but we're going to have to watch him.'

'Understood, Doc.' Baz was no novice to the job. He knew well the battle that had been fought here and for the moment won. 'Right, let's get this youngster on his way, then. If you're ready, Liam, on my count.'

In unison they gently rolled Nathan first on one side and then the other, sliding each section of the supporting plinth under him and snapping the pieces together. A sturdy rope was attached to each end of the stretcher and soon it was being winched safely to the top.

With Baz departing as well, Liam stared down at Nikki, his gaze warm. 'Well done, you.'

'Oh, Liam…' To her disgust she folded like a wet tissue. She went to him and hugged him, beating back a new avalanche of tears. 'I hate this part of being a doctor.'

'I know. It's rough.' He rubbed his chin on the top of her head. 'We'd better make tracks, though. Nathan has to be our main priority until we hand him over to the CareFlight crew.' He bent and hitched up the trauma pack. 'I'm parched. Let's hope there's some tea left in one of those flasks.'

Nikki blocked a yawn. 'Perhaps Michelle made only coffee.'

He dragged up an exaggerated sigh from his boots. 'Then I guess I'll just have to cope, won't I?'

'It's after midnight.' Nikki made the observation as they stood, tracking the blinking lights of the aircraft across the pale night sky.

Nathan was on his way to hospital. His family had been notified and would be on hand to meet the flight.

Danny had offered Joel a bed, promising they'd be up at first light to locate his car. After the rather abortive end to their holiday, Joel had made it clear he didn't want to hang about. He'd gather up the rest of the gear from their campsite and begin the long drive back to Brisbane.

'Ready to go?' Liam slung his arm across Nikki's shoulders and they turned, making their way across to where the Land Rover was parked on the periphery of the airstrip.

'Won't take us long to get home.'

They were quiet as they drove. Nikki clasped her hands in her lap, conscious of an odd kind of tension knotting the air between them.

When they arrived home, they kicked off their shoes and trooped through to the kitchen. Nikki made a face at the unwashed dishes. 'Like something to eat?'

'No, thanks.' Liam opened a top cupboard. 'I just need a drink. You take the shower first.'

Feeling dismissed, Nikki turned and left. He hadn't invited her to share a drink with him, she fumed, peeling off her soiled clothes and shoving them into the hamper.

They hadn't even debriefed properly, for heaven's sake! He could have spared her a few of his precious minutes, surely. She climbed into the shower, letting the hot stream of water ease her aching muscles, then realised she'd stayed far too long.

Guiltily, she closed off the taps. One slip-up didn't constitute a major crime, she told her conscience defensively. Returning to her bedroom, she cast the towel aside, slipping on a simple T-shirt nightie. Then she plonked down on the edge of the bed, memories bombarding her out of nowhere.

Memories of when she and Liam had had the privilege of sharing a bed, waking in the night and reaching for each other. Memories of murmured words
and soft sighs of fulfilment. Other memories of a
wild coming together that had left them breathless
and shaken.

She ran her hands roughly through her hair as if
to clear away the shards of retrospection, deciding
that reminiscing was fruitless. At one time she and
Liam had had a marriage. And now neither of them
seemed to know whether or not they wanted it back.
Or, if they did, how to go about it. Sighing, she
stood. She needed a glass of water.

Barefoot, she padded along to the kitchen, wondering fleetingly if Liam was still there or whether
perhaps he'd taken his drink and gone out onto the
deck. Well, wherever he was, he clearly didn't want
her company. She'd get her water and take herself
off to bed.

But several seconds later all her noble intentions
fell flat on their collective faces. At the door of the
kitchen she paused and drew back. Liam was seated
at the table, looking down into his glass of whisky,
a look of absolute bleakness on his face, a muscle
working overtime in his jaw.

Nikki took a shaken breath, barely resisting the
urge to go to him, to take the glass out of his hand
and simply hold him.

Oh, lord. Her hand went to her heart. He was so
tense. Like a bowstring that had been stretched too
tight and was about to snap. Her teeth clenched on
her bottom lip and she took a step back. For a second

she stood there and then she brought her head up and decided to throw caution to the winds.

'Liam…'

He lifted his head, blinking as if he needed to focus.

'You OK?' Nikki felt her heart begin to thud in slow, suffocatingly heavy strokes as she covered the short distance to stand beside him.

He looked up at her, his expression slightly glazed. 'I ache a bit. Long old day.'

'Let me help.'

He held up the whisky bottle which was more than half-full. 'Even between the two of us, that might take a while.'

Nikki lifted her gaze briefly. 'Not that. Let me ease the tension out of your shoulders.'

'A massage?'

'I still know how,' she reminded him.

'I don't doubt it.' He laughed shortly. 'But is it wise?'

'Oh, for heaven's sake!' Leaning forward, she snapped open several buttons on his shirt and tugged it over his head. 'Now, relax,' she ordered, running her fingers experimentally over the planes of his shoulders and into the deep cord of muscle at the base of his neck. After a minute she huffed, 'This is hopeless. You're as tight as a drum. I'll get some oil.'

She came back bearing a small brown bottle.

Liam eyed it suspiciously. 'What is it?'

Nikki poured some of the oil into her palm. 'It's a blend of lavender, almond and myrrh and a couple of others. Now, close your eyes and try to let go.'

Methodically, she smoothed the oil over his skin and began all over again, working her fingers deep into the areas where she could feel his muscles grabbing, her whole being concentrating on the rhythm of her hands.

'Now we're getting somewhere,' she murmured with satisfaction, feeling his muscles beginning to unknot under her smoothing and kneading. Suddenly the thought crept in that the whole process she was engaged in was almost erotic.

Her heart gave a dangerous little skip. She took in a steadying breath, acknowledging the rapid acceleration of her pulse, relishing the warm smoothness of his skin, and how touching him like this was heaping pleasure on her senses...

'Enough.' Suddenly Liam reached back to still her hands. 'That's fine. Thanks...'

'Oh—OK.' She frowned slightly. Such gratitude. She lifted her hands away and stood back. 'Fine.' She went across to the bench, her back to him as she tore off a section of paper towel to wipe her hands.

'Nikki?'

She turned, crunching the paper towel and dropping it into the bin. 'Liam?'

'Thank you,' he began throatily. 'I mean that—it was fantastic. But...I shouldn't have let you do it to me.'

Nikki's gaze widened. 'Why ever not?'

'Because...' A gravelly sigh dragged itself up from the depths of his chest. 'Because it's too intimate.'

'Oh.' She felt her face flood with colour. She tried to swallow but the action seemed too complicated.

Instead, she licked her lips. 'I didn't mean to embarrass you—you looked so tense. I just— I'm sorry.'

'No, don't apologise. Please.' He held out a hand to her and she took it, allowing him to draw her closer.

'You could have stopped me.' She sank weakly onto his lap.

His fingers, blunt and strong, tipped her chin up gently so that she met his eyes. They were dark pools. Fathoms deep. 'I'm a masochist, I suppose.' His mouth pulled down in a mocking little twist. 'And your hands delivered such exquisite torture.'

'Did they just…?' Nikki moved a bit uncomfortably on his lap. She knew that already. 'So, Dr Donovan…' She began edging closer, pressing against him, her mouth barely a breath away from his.

'So, what?'

He'd spoken quietly, his voice so deep it made her shiver. 'You must know what,' she murmured, raising her hands, spreading her fingers to bracket his face. 'I think I deserve payment, don't you?'

He tasted of whisky and his jaw was rough with new beard. Their mouths sought each other's, sipped and nipped, and she heard a half-growl escape from his throat as their kiss deepened.

I don't want to be alone tonight, she whispered silently. And it would be so easy. A few steps along the hallway to her—*his* bedroom. And it was what she wanted, needed.

She felt him pulling back, his fingers moving to twine in her hair at the back. The gentlest pressure brought her head up. His eyes, disturbingly dark, looked into her face. 'Nikki…' His throat worked as he swallowed. 'We can't take this any further.'

'Why not?' She was kissing him again, touching him, her fingers working their way down over his throat, his chest, across the hard male nipples. 'I want you…' Her mouth dallied with his again, meltingly soft against his. 'Liam, want me too…'

'No!' Liam recoiled. 'Nikki, we have to stop.' His eyes smouldering, he looked into her face. 'Right now.'

'Why?' She swallowed heavily, her mind half-numb. 'We could be reconciled. Don't you want that?'

'Oh, sweet,' he muttered hoarsely, nuzzling the side of her head. 'It's been a hell of a day. We're both strung out and emotional. It's not the right time to make such far-reaching decisions.'

She felt her head drop a little. 'You don't want me.'

'On the contrary,' he refuted, nudging a strand of her hair sideways, seeking the soft skin behind her ear. 'You drive me crazy.'

Nikki's head tipped to one side. 'Then why are you holding back?'

His hands slid beneath her. 'I told you why.' He levered himself upright taking her with him. 'Plus— and this probably sounds a bit lame—I don't have any protection about the place.'

'Oh, Liam…' She took one of his hands, raising it to her mouth to kiss his knuckles. 'That tells me so much about you.'

His eyes narrowed. 'It does?'

'Mmm.' She draped her arms around his waist. 'It tells me you haven't had a woman here in ages.'

He laughed—a short painful sound—brushing her cheek with the tip of one finger. 'Lady, I haven't *had* a woman in ages.'

Wherever else they might have gone with the conversation was never realised. Instead, they were distracted by Lightning. Tail whipping importantly, he ambled into the kitchen and parked himself at their feet. He looked up, his green eyes asking for approval.

'Aagh!' Nikki shrieked. 'He's got a mouse!'

Liam looked amused. 'For crying out loud, Nik, he's a cat! He's showing us how clever he is.'

'I don't want to know.' She put her hand to her throat. 'Is it dead?'

'Very, I should think.'

Nikki crossed her arms, her fingers pulling agitatedly at the edges of her sleeves. 'Can you dispose of it, please?'

'Wimp.' Liam chuckled. 'Go to bed.' He flicked a hand to shoo her away. 'I'll see to it.'

'Good.' She stepped delicately away. 'I don't want to find it decorating the place in the morning. Uh, Liam…' She paused at the door and looked back. 'If you should…change your mind, I won't be asleep.'

Liam tilted his head, meeting her regard levelly. 'Good night, Nikki.'

In other words, no chance. She spun on her heel and walked away.

'Stubborn man.' She hugged her arms around her shoulders and rocked herself gently in the middle of the bed. Whatever made you think you could influence him, Nicola? And as for talking him into bed…

Eyes sparkling with unshed tears and exhausted by emotion, she climbed between the sheets. One day soon, she promised herself. Gathering the pillow to her, she snuggled against the cool cotton fabric and imagined how it would be when she and Liam were lovers again.

CHAPTER EIGHT

NIKKI was heartened when Sonia Reed kept her promise to bring Emily in for a check-up before the family left Wirilda next morning. And now, having examined the child, she'd asked Grace to keep her occupied while she had a chat to the young mother.

'Apart from the eczema, Sonia, Emily seems a healthy child.'

'That's good to hear.' Sonia turned an anxious eye towards the door. 'She'll be OK with the receptionist, won't she?' She spread her hands in appeal. 'It's just that she doesn't really get a chance to mix with anyone outside the immediate family.'

Nikki sent her a reassuring smile. 'Grace has a knack with kids. She'll keep her entertained. And I really wanted this time to speak privately with you.'

Sonia nodded. 'I've used the oat sock in the bath,' she confided eagerly. 'I know it's too soon to see any results…'

'But it's a start,' Nikki said approvingly. 'Have you thought any further about getting Emily to a dietitian?'

The young woman flushed slightly. 'Actually, I had a long talk to Marcus last night after the show. Oddly enough, we'd both been thinking along the same lines—that we'd like to leave the circus and get a more settled lifestyle.'

'So, is it going to be a possibility?' Nikki asked gently.

'We hope so.' Sonia raised a shoulder. 'It'll depend on whether his dad can afford some kind of severance package. Marc deserves something,' she said loyally. 'He's worked in the circus since he left school and has always given his best. And I've pulled my weight, too, wherever I could. Sorry.' She bit her lips together. 'I know you must be busy and I'm rattling on.'

'You're my last appointment before lunch,' Nikki said kindly. 'I can spare a few minutes. So…' she said consideringly. 'Providing you and your husband can come to some satisfactory arrangement, you could be settled quite soon?'

'I'd like to think so. We'll head back east towards one of the regional cities. I'd love to be able to start Em at kindergarten or playgroup. And Marc will get work,' she added with the confidence of youth. 'He may have to retrain for something but I can work while he does that. I was a school secretary. That's how we met. Marc came in one day to leave some free passes for the students…'

The consultation finally came to an end. 'Good luck with everything.' Nikki stood at the door of her surgery and warmly bade Sonia farewell.

'Thanks, Dr Barrett—I mean thanks for listening and putting me on the right track about Em. The mums at the laundrette were right about you.' Sonia gave a nervous little laugh, her fingers fluttering to the medallion at her throat. 'You really are tuned in to your patients.'

Feeling upbeat and appreciated, Nikki made her

way along to the lunch-room. Liam was already seated, his head buried in a medical journal.

'Hi,' she said, her confidence fading slightly. He looked tired and grim. 'You were gone early this morning.'

'Call-out,' he responded without lifting his gaze. 'One of the elderly ladies from the nursing home went on a wander. The night sister wanted her checked over. Busy surgery?' He finally raised his head, flipping the journal closed.

'As always.' Nikki pulled out a chair and sat opposite him. She put out a hand, stroking it along his forearm. 'Did you get much sleep?'

Liam didn't respond.

'I mean it would be understandable if you didn't...' The words tumbled out and then she slowly withdrew her hand, cross with herself for referring even obliquely to the new level of intimacy they'd reached last night.

Finally, Liam said carefully, 'Nikki, where are you going with this?'

Her eyes widened. It wasn't the reaction she'd expected at all. 'I...only wanted to talk about things— about us.'

He blinked. 'Now isn't the time.'

Nettled, she asked bluntly, 'When will be the time, then?'

He made a throw-away motion with his hand.

'Then should I make an appointment with you?' she retorted, deliberately facetious.

'You're being childish,' he drawled darkly.

She looked at him for a long moment, then said

steadily, 'If our relationship is such a trial to you, perhaps I'd better move out.'

He hooted. 'Give me a break. Where would you go?'

She shrugged. 'I don't know—the pub?'

'I'm not having you living there, Nikki, so just forget it.'

'Don't tell me what to do!'

'Stop this,' he rasped urgently. 'Grace will be here any second and I won't have our personal affairs—'

'Who's having an affair?' Grace bustled in with a loaded lunch-tray, her gaze bright with curiosity.

Nikki snorted. 'No one around here, that's for sure.'

Liam's eyes narrowed on her flushed face, the angry tilt of her small chin. Damn! There was so much he'd *wanted* to say to her. Was he being an over-cautious clod? It was clear where Nikki had wanted last night to end.

He lifted a hand, spanning his temple, massaging an obvious ache. Maybe that's what he should do—take her to bed and to hell with the consequences. He took a deep controlling breath and managed a passable smile. 'You're a lifesaver, Gracie. Sit down. I'll pour the tea.'

Grace needed no second invitation. 'I heard some rather disturbing news this morning.' Her faintly troubled eyes linked the two doctors. 'The primary school is about to lose a chunk of its teacher aide funding.'

'How come?' Nikki took a sandwich and made an effort to concentrate.

'Well...' Grace was already in full flight. 'Over

the past few weeks two more families have had to leave the district. They each had two children at the school.'

'So the school is now down four students.' Keeping his gaze firmly averted, Liam placed a mug of tea in front of Nikki.

Grace nodded. 'And places mean funding. For heaven's sake, it's five precious hours a week that's being lost to the students, to say nothing of the drop in her annual salary for the teacher aide.'

'That's Jade Murphy, isn't it?' Liam's mouth drew in. 'I play squash with her husband Damien sometimes. Any idea of the salary cut?'

'Around the four thousand dollar mark,' Grace said gloomily. 'But it may as well be four million.'

'Why don't we organise a community effort to raise the money?' Nikki brightened at the new challenge. 'Perhaps a quick mega-raffle. Surely if we club together we could come up with a suitable prize.'

'It would be like robbing Peter to pay Paul.' Liam dismissed her idea. 'No one's got any spare cash to buy raffle tickets.'

Nikki swallowed through a hard little laugh. 'Well, that's me shot down in flames.'

'Oh, Nikki, it was a lovely thought.' Sensing the tension between the two, Grace rushed in to restore calm. 'But Liam's right.' She shook her head. 'There's really nothing we can do.'

Nikki took a thoughtful swallow of her tea. She didn't believe in giving up so easily. She was part of this small community now. There had to be *something* they could do.

'But on the other hand...' Grace, it seemed, had more information to convey. 'I heard some good news this morning as well.' She paused for effect. 'Bernie Hardy's been appointed as the new manager for the caravan park. He's positively bursting with pride. And you, Doctor...' she laughingly aimed an index finger at Nikki '...encouraged him to apply, I believe?'

Nikki huffed a dismissive laugh. 'I made a couple of phone calls, that's all. Bernie got the job on his merits.'

Liam straightened slowly, narrowing a questioning look at her. 'Sounds like community medicine at its best. You're full of surprises, Nikki. As always.'

Nikki returned to her consulting room to take her afternoon clinic. She felt miserable. Why did she let Liam rock her equilibrium like this?

She went across to the window and stood staring out at the marigolds and nasturtiums blooming bravely despite the harsh climatic conditions.

She sighed. Even the plants were making an effort to hold on, to finish what they'd begun. She and Liam couldn't even seem to make a beginning...

The harsh ring of the telephone jarred her senses. Inhaling a ragged little breath, Nikki yanked herself back to the real world. She slipped into her chair and picked up the phone.

'Nicola Barrett.'

'Oh, Nikki, it's Wendy Palmer from the child-care centre. I think we've huge trouble on our hands.'

Nikki's hand tightened on the receiver. Wendy was the centre's director and from what Nikki could judge, after just a couple of visits to the centre, she didn't appear to be the panicky type. 'OK, Wendy, slow down. What kind of trouble are we talking about here?'

'Meningococcal.'

Just the sound of the word sent a cold river of dread flooding down Nikki's spine. 'Who's affected and what are the symptoms?'

'One of the babies. We've been concerned about her for the last little while. Now she's developed a kind of light, pink-spotted rash—'

'Is the rash smudgy or small?' Nikki rapped.

'Small. Her temperature's up and she's screaming the place down. Oh, Nikki, it's hell on wheels here.'

Nikki was already on her feet. 'Get hold of the parents, Wendy. It's imperative.'

'We've been trying since Taylor seemed so unwell. But the mother's mobile is switched off and there's no father on the scene. Oh—hang on a minute, Nikki.'

Nikki heard the sound of agitated voices and then Wendy was back on the line. 'My workers have just informed me two of their toddler group are displaying similar symptoms. What should we do?'

'Stay put. No one is to go in or out of the centre unless we authorise it, Wendy. And that's an order.'

'Yes—yes, I understand.'

Mentally Nikki crossed her fingers as she asked the next question. 'Have you and the staff all had your vaccinations against meningococcal?'

'Yes.'

'Liam and I will be straight there. And, Wendy,

have the three affected children's health particulars ready, please.'

Nikki slammed the phone down, personal problems shoved aside as she sped across the corridor to Liam's room. She burst in without knocking. 'Emergency at the child-care centre. We're needed over there.' Using medical shorthand, she took only a few seconds to fill him in.

'Right.' Liam hefted his bag and tore ahead of her out of the room. 'Grab what vaccinations we have, please. I'll give Grace a few instructions, then wait in the car for you. Run, Nikki. These minutes could be crucial.'

Nikki ran.

At Reception, Liam began giving a stream of orders to Grace. 'Ring the hospital. Speak to Anna and tell her we have an emergency at the child-care centre. We need her and another nurse to meet us there. Ask her bring all their available meningococcal vaccine and a paediatrics trauma kit. And we need both ambulances on standby and someone waiting in Pathology.'

Grace snatched up the phone. 'Should I cancel all appointments for this afternoon?'

'Please.' Liam hauled the door open. 'This could take the rest of the day.'

'Not a good feeling, is it?' With Nikki on board, Liam reversed the Land Rover in a swift arc.

'No.' Nikki searched his grim profile. 'I had the slender hope it could have been measles. We'll have to notify the health department.'

'We'll do that as soon as we've confirmed it's meningococcal. Just let's hope we can contain it.'

Nikki bit down on her bottom lip. 'Children are so vulnerable, aren't they?'

'The very young and the very old,' Liam agreed, and his voice sounded throaty.

Anna and Michelle arrived at the centre within seconds of the doctors. Wendy met them at the door. 'We've put the baby in the sick bay and isolated the two toddlers in the small playroom,' she said without preamble. 'I've checked all three children's enrolment details. No allergic reactions are listed.'

'Thanks, Wendy. That's brilliant.' Liam strode between the rows of little mattresses on the floor. 'Nikki and I will do the baby first. And, Anna, if you and Michelle will check on the toddlers and report back to us?'

'You'll find them in there.' Wendy pointed the nurses towards the small playroom.

'Where are the other children?' Nikki's gaze swept the empty room.

Wendy lifted a hand and rubbed a finger across her temple. 'They're on the back verandah. I've sent Rosie to read to them and do whatever else she can to keep them occupied.' The director gave a strained smile. 'Thank heavens for those little puppets you left here on your last visit, Nikki!'

Nikki nodded. 'Just remember, Wendy, no one is to be allowed in or out until we say so.'

Wendy put a hand to her throat. 'Some of the parents will be arriving soon to collect their children.'

'Make a sign quickly and hang it outside. If they've mobiles, they'll probably ring so be ready with your answers. We'll give you more information as soon as we can.'

Nikki almost sprinted along the corridor to the sick bay. 'We'll take over now,' she said gently to the young worker who was standing beside the little change table, looking down at the baby.

'She's very ill.'

'Yes, she is.' Nikki's heart ached for the young worker, whose name badge proclaimed she was called Cathy.

'I've looked after her since she's been coming to the centre.'

'We'll do all we can,' Nikki promised. 'Meanwhile, could you help the two nurses with the sick toddlers, please?'

Cathy cast a lingering look at the baby and then left.

'She's unconscious, Nikki.' Liam was checking the child's vital signs as he spoke. 'Temperature's way up, 39, fast pulse and rapid respiration rates.'

Nikki pulled up the tiny T-shirt and loosened the nappy. 'The rash appears to have spread all over. Let's get her on oxygen, Liam. I'd say six litres per minute. Will you do the IV? We need to get fluids and an antibiotic into her.'

Because all young children tended to thrash their arms about, Liam deftly slid the cannula into the infant's ankle.

'Anything I can do to help?' Wendy appeared at the door.

'Some wet towels, please.' Liam was quickly drawing up the dose of antibiotics. 'We need to get her temperature down.'

'Coming up.' Wendy left at a run.

'What are you giving her?' Nikki swabbed the cannula in readiness.

'Vancomycin. That seems to be the consensus in Paeds at the moment. There you are, little one,' he said softly, as he injected the antibiotic, willing the tiny vein to begin carrying the lifesaving drug to every part of the infant's body.

Michelle stuck her head in the door. 'Both toddlers have high temps and rash. Cathy's presently running a bath and we'll start sponging them. We'll be ready when you're free to cannulate. I should warn you, you'll need all your skills, they're very distressed.'

'Thanks, Michelle,' Liam acknowledged with a grim twist to his mouth. 'We should be through here shortly. Ambulance arrived?'

'Just pulled up, someone said. And they could only send one, unfortunately.'

'Liam!' Nikki's alarm tore through the room. 'She's fitting! Valium, quick!' The baby's eyes were rolling back in her head and she was beginning to stiffen.

'Hold her!' Liam's reaction was instantaneous. He grabbed for the drugs pack. They were working frantically against time but in seconds he'd drawn up the infant dosage and sent it home.

'I've increased the oxygen to eight litres per minute.' Nikki's heart was in her mouth. They couldn't lose this little one. They just couldn't!

'Thirty seconds.' Liam monitored his watch. 'Damn! She should be coming out of it.'

'She is.' Nikki's heart returned to its rightful place. 'The drug's working. She's stopping. Oh, thank God…'

Liam's face remained grim. 'We don't have a minute to spare, Nikki. We have to get this infant to hospital. I'll have to leave you to manage the toddlers.'

Nikki knew time was of the essence but before they could proceed any further the path lab would have to run a blood test to confirm the meningococcal virus. 'Go. I'll start working on the toddlers.'

'Can you manage?' A frown creased Liam's forehead.

Nikki hefted her case and the trauma pack. 'With Anna and Michelle to help me, of course. Send the ambulance back as soon as you can.'

Liam looked torn. 'I'll try to get back if I can.'

'Just save that baby.' She waved him out. 'I'll cope.'

'This isn't over by a long shot, Nikki,' Liam warned.

'I'm aware of that,' she snapped, the strain of the past twenty-four hours catching up with her. There were a mountain of tasks yet to be completed. Vaccination of all the children attending the day-care centre plus their parents and siblings.

And it would all have to be done today.

The toddlers were screaming. 'The sponging's helped to bring the temps down a bit.' Anna struggled to hold one of the children as he arched back and fought for freedom from the confining arms.

Nikki took in the scene, her mind sharp and practical. 'We need some triage here, guys. Michelle, put your toddler in the cot for a second and give Anna and Cathy a hand to hold this little man. There's no way I can get an IV in with him thrashing about like a wounded bull calf.'

That analogy brought the semblance of a smile from the team. 'I hope you've got nimble fingers, Nikki!' Anna raised her voice above the din.

Nikki worked instinctively, her movements swift and sure. In seconds the cannula was in and holding. 'Right, that's number one. We'll run in normal saline and I'll administer the antibiotic. As soon as I've done that, Michelle, I want you to bandage the IV firmly so this little chap can't kick out the line.'

The second toddler was a sturdy little girl who fought tooth and nail against the procedure and consequently the whole thing took longer. Finally it was done.

'Now, let's get them both on oxygen, please,' Nikki instructed. 'Run it at four litres per minute.'

Nikki was still hard at work when Wendy appeared at the door. 'Liam just called.' Her face had taken on a pinched look. 'The lab rushed through the blood test. It's confirmed meningococcal.'

Well, it was what they'd thought—and dreaded. Nikki felt her nerve-ends tighten to a hard knot in her stomach. 'Right, then. From this moment the centre is quarantined.'

'Oh.' Wendy made a tiny sound of dismay and bit her lips together. 'The rest of the children will have to be vaccinated, won't they?'

'They will,' Nikki agreed. 'But first we're going to need the parents' consent. So, Wendy, you'd better have your staff begin working the phones.'

'We've only the one line.' The director looked aghast. 'But most of us have mobile phones.'

'Good. Use them and I'll see you're all reimbursed for the calls. And remind the parents they'll have to present themselves here for vaccination, along with any siblings of the children here at the centre. But they'll have to remain outside. I'm sure we can get a tent or something put up and some chairs sent over.'

'The SES will have it in hand,' Michelle said confidently. 'And one of the church groups will organise hot drinks and sandwiches as a matter of course.'

'I've managed to contact the mothers of the children at risk,' Wendy said. 'I've told them to go straight to the hospital.'

'Thanks for all your help, Wendy.' Nikki began packing up her case. 'I'll leave Anna and Michelle here to begin the vaccinations but I need to get these two little people to hospital. We'll keep in touch.'

The infant and the toddlers had been placed in the tiny isolation ward, all confirmed as having the meningococcal virus.

'I've made arrangements to medivac them to the Royal Children's this evening,' Liam told Nikki. His brow furrowed. 'Let's hope they all pull through.'

'What about the parents?' Nikki's mind flew ahead. 'Are they going to be able to accompany their little ones?'

'They're making arrangements now. And the Royal has parent accommodation nearby so that's one less thing they'll have to worry about.'

'Mmm.' Nikki glanced at her watch. 'I should get back to the child-care centre and begin taking the bloods. Our lab is not going to be able to cope with the testing, though, Liam.'

'We'll send the samples back with the CareFlight people. One of the Brisbane labs will work through the night and knock them off in no time. We should have the results back as early as tomorrow morning. Right.' He folded his stethoscope and placed it to one side. 'Let's get back to the centre.'

Nikki's gaze widened in query. 'I thought you'd want to stay and monitor the children.'

Liam shook his head. 'One of the senior nurses can do that. Anna's called in all staff to help out. Even Dion offered to dust off her nursing skills if we need her.'

Nikki blocked a yawn. 'Good for her.'

Outside in the car park once more, they piled into the Land Rover. 'You've been magnificent through this, Nik,' Liam murmured, his voice husky.

Nikki drew an unsteady breath. 'You've been pretty inspiring yourself.' Their eyes met for an intense moment before each looked uncomfortably away.

When they arrived back at the centre, Nikki went in search of Anna. Two more nurses had come to help out but nevertheless Anna and Michelle must be out on their feet, she thought worriedly. 'How's it going?' She'd finally tracked the charge nurse down at the end of a long line of people.

'We've just about finished the jabs.' Lifting her forearm, Anna brushed a strand of hair away from her forehead. 'Are you and Liam going to do the bloods?'

'Yes.' Nikki went on to explain the arrangements that had been made to fly the samples to Brisbane for testing. Her gaze flew over the group of anxious faces. 'How have folk coped through all this, Anna?'

Anna smothered a dry laugh. 'Apart from complaining that the tea was either too hot or not hot enough, they've been quite stoic, really. But, oh, lord, what a day!'

They were home at last.

Nikki got stiffly out of the Land Rover and stretched. Tipping her head up, she peered at the trees. 'Is that actually a moist little breeze I can feel?'

Liam dropped a hand on her shoulder. 'Perhaps it's a forerunner of rain.'

Her eyes flew wide. 'Could it be?'

'Anything's possible, as they say.' He turned her towards him and searched her face in the dim light. 'You OK?'

'Yes—once I've had my shower and washed today's events down the plughole. How about you?'

His mouth tipped into a crooked smile. 'A bit rough, actually.' He drew her into his arms and rested his head against hers. 'I know I keep saying it, but you were magnificent today, Nikki.'

Nikki pulled back and made a face at him. 'Flattery at this time of night will get you nowhere, Doctor.'

He laughed and hugged her. 'Once you get cleaned up and have a sleep, you'll feel better.' He walked her towards the front door, opened it and pushed her gently inside.

Almost stumbling with exhaustion, Nikki made

her way along the hallway to her bedroom. A few minutes later, showered and with her hair briefly dried, she fell into bed. She was asleep in seconds.

Next morning dawned bright and clear with no hint of rain. Nikki gave a rueful smile. Perhaps, she'd imagined her moist breeze. Automatically, she dropped bread in the toaster.

'I've just been on to the Royal,' Liam announced, coming through to the kitchen. 'Our three little people are holding their own.'

'Oh, thank goodness!' Nikki's hand flew to her heart. 'Anything yet on the bloods?'

'Later this morning, they said.' He sent her a trapped smile. 'But no one's called in with any symptoms so far. If we end up with just the three cases, it'll be nothing short of a miracle.'

Nikki rescued the bacon from under the grill. 'Miracles happen all the time. Didn't you know?'

CHAPTER NINE

IT WAS with some surprise Nikki noted the name of her last patient for the day. 'You're the teacher aide at the school, aren't you?'

'Fancy you knowing that!' Jade Murphy tinkled a laugh, touching a hand to her cloud of auburn hair.

Nikki waved her to a chair. 'How can I help you today, Jade?'

The young woman made a small face. 'Actually, I feel a bit of fraud coming here. But I'd made the appointment...' She trailed off and looked down at her hands.

'I heard about your work hours being cut.' Nikki's quiet statement filled the vacuum.

'The whole town will have heard by now.' Jade raised stricken eyes. 'This drought is having a domino effect right throughout the district. One thing happens and it goes on and on right down the line.'

'The times are very difficult,' Nikki agreed. 'Liam and I see it all the time in our practice. But I'm sure you didn't come in today to discuss the drought.'

'Ah...no. Damien and I want to try for a baby.' She stopped, rolling her bottom lip between her teeth. 'But now with my wage cut, perhaps it isn't the greatest time to be thinking about it.'

'Well, that's for you both to decide,' Nikki said diplomatically. 'Did you plan on having a check-up today? Ask some questions about getting pregnant and so on?'

'Yes, I did. But would I be wasting your time if we didn't go ahead?'

'Of course not.' Nikki smiled. 'And as you're here anyway…'

'OK. Where should we start?'

'Well, I'll need some history.' Nikki looked down at Jade's card. 'Except for renewing your script for the Pill, you don't seem to have much here.'

'We haven't been in Wirilda that long. I think I've only been in for a couple of minor things. And I had a flu shot because of working around the kids. Sorry.' She tossed Nikki an apologetic glance. 'I'll stop waffling and get to the point.'

'Perhaps we could start by my giving you a general outline of the various steps necessary to begin preparing your body for pregnancy?' Nikki suggested.

'Oh, could you?' Jade leaned forward eagerly. 'That would be fantastic.'

Nikki took up her pen. 'So, how long have you been taking the Pill, Jade?'

'All up, about five years. I have to confess I'm a bit concerned about any side-effects after I stop taking it. I mean, you hear all kinds of stories, don't you?'

'And many of them are embellished along the way.' Nikki's response held a note of caution. 'But it is a fact the Pill can rob your body of certain vitamins and minerals,' she agreed. 'So, to begin with, we'll test your iron levels, for the simple reason that blood volume increases with pregnancy and anaemia is fairly common.'

'I understand. And someone told me I'd need a pap smear. I'm a real wimp about them,' Jade confessed with wry honesty.

Nikki husked a laugh. 'As females, we all tend to avoid them, but they're all we have at the moment to detect anything untoward. And if it's two years since you've had one then, yes, we'd need to do that. We'd also need to take blood to check your immunity to rubella and chickenpox. Do you smoke, Jade?'

'No, never have. That's good, isn't it?'

'Brilliant. And if you're serious about becoming pregnant, you should give alcohol and caffeine a miss or at least cut back.'

Jade nodded. 'And what about diet and stuff?'

'Lots of fresh fruit and veg, of course,' Nikki said. 'And if you start taking a folic acid supplement three months or so before conception, it's very beneficial.'

'I've heard about that. What's the idea of it exactly?'

'It lessens the incidence of specific defects in the foetus. I can give you some literature that covers the relevant points.'

'Then I guess I have to ask the sixty-four-thousand-dollar question.' Jade gave a shy little smile. 'How soon could I expect to get pregnant after I stopped taking the Pill?'

'There are some figures on this.' Nikki tapped a few keys on her computer and read off the screen. 'OK—ten per cent of couples conceive in the first month after stopping the Pill, sixty by six months and ninety by twelve months. That's assuming both you and your partner are healthy.'

Jade laughed a little breathlessly. 'It makes the possibility sound so real. But there's quite a lot to think about, isn't there? And once you're pregnant, there's no going back and you have to hang in there for a whole nine months...'

'But just think,' Nikki told her with a grin. 'At the end of your nine-month journey, you reap a wonderful reward.'

'Yes, there's that.' Jade's look was soft. 'I guess I'd better talk all this over with Damien before we go any further.' She glanced at her watch and then met Nikki's gaze with a slight smile. 'But I suppose I could have the dreaded pap smear now, if you've time?'

'All the time in the world.' Nikki got to her feet. 'Just strip everything off from the waist down, please, Jade, and pop up on the couch. That's lovely.' Nikki unfurled a modesty sheet and pulled the screen around her patient. A few minutes later she placed the specimen on the slide. 'There now. Wasn't too bad, was it?'

Her patient gave a cracked laugh. 'I've had worse. But, no, you're a pretty smooth operator.'

'Then you won't mind if I do a quick internal check while you're here? Just to make sure everything is where it should be?'

'It makes sense, I suppose.' Jade bit down on the underside of her lip. 'And if I'm going to try for a baby, I guess I'd better get used to being examined.'

'That's very positive.' Nikki sent her an approving

smile. 'I'll just label this for despatch and be right back.'

As Jade was her last patient, Nikki walked out to Reception with her after the examination. 'The result of your smear should be back within a week.'

'Oh—OK.' Jade touched a hand to the frilly neckline of her top. 'May I call you during surgery hours to find out?'

'That's fine.' Nikki pulled open the heavy plate-glass front door. 'Good luck with everything.'

Jade lifted a hand, curling a strand of auburn hair around her finger. 'I have a feeling Damien will want to go ahead, despite my job being uncertain. Otherwise, well, you could wait for ever.'

Nikki nodded. 'I know what you mean. Isn't there a proverb or something that suggests if we wait until the wind and the rain are just right, we won't achieve anything?'

Jade gave a snip of laughter. 'Probably. Anyway, I'd best be on my way and let you go on yours. Thanks for everything, Dr Barrett.'

'You're welcome.' Nikki's smile was warm. 'And, please, call me, Nikki. We'll probably be old friends before too long if I'm to see you through this baby business.'

'I'll be in touch, then, Nikki. Thanks again.'

Now, there's a lady who knows where she's going, Nikki thought, her look faintly wistful as she watched her patient's swift, purposeful stride across the street to her car.

'Call from Sydney for you, Nikki.' Grace held the receiver aloft, her hand over the mouthpiece. 'A

Simon Dennison. I said I'd see if you were available.'

Nikki returned Jade's fluttered wave as she drove off, turning from the door with a small sigh. 'It's fine, Grace, he's an old friend. I'll take it in my office, thanks.'

'Hi, Simon.' Nikki pushed enthusiasm into her voice and thought of their two different worlds. 'How's my favourite stockbroker these days?'

'Haven't been hung out to dry yet, Nikki. How's the surgical-glove business? On seconds thoughts, don't answer that.' Simon Dennison's relaxed chuckle came smoothly down the line. 'I have a proposition for you.'

'Now you're talking!'

'Cheeky monkey. I'm a married man.'

Nikki's mouth curled on a laugh. 'Then you shouldn't go around propositioning young women, should you? What's up? You haven't called to tell me I've gone bust, have you?' Feeling entirely at ease with the friend from her high-school years, she settled in for a chat, wriggling her bottom into a more comfortable position in the chair.

'Far from it. Your shares in Salvin Gold have taken a huge hike. I think you should sell.'

'OK.' Nikki didn't even have to think about it. She'd always trusted Simon to steer her right when it came to her share portfolio.

'And reinvest?'

'Ah…' Her gaze snapped up, as Liam knocked and poked his head in. She beckoned him in and resumed her phone conversation. 'What kind of results are we talking about here, Simon?'

'Ten big ones.'

'Oh, my goodness.' Nikki's hand went to her heart. 'That's amazing.'

'Not bad.' Simon was neutral. 'Nikki, I have to move fast on this so should I reinvest?'

She thought quickly. 'Half only.'

'And the rest in your bank?'

'Yes, please.'

'Not a problem. I'm right on it. *Ciao*.'

'Bye, Simon. Thanks.' Nikki replaced the receiver carefully and brought her head up, looking directly at Liam.

'Who's Simon?' His moody gaze raked her face.

Nikki thought briefly of telling him to mind his own business but relented. It didn't matter anyway. 'My stockbroker.'

He went very still, all his energies reined in. Then he looked at her mutely and shook his head.

'What?' Her dark brows flexed impatiently.

He gave a hard-edged laugh. 'You're obviously still wheeling and dealing.'

A flood of colour washed over her cheeks. He'd made it sound almost an insult. 'I don't make money my god the way my father did,' she snapped.

He made a soft sound. 'I didn't say you did, Nikki.'

'Your look spoke a thousand words, Liam.'

'Then I apologise.'

'You still have me pegged as a chip off the old block, don't you?'

'Your words, Nikki.'

Her hand tightened around the paperweight on her desk and she lowered her gaze, remembering how many fights they'd had over just that. But these days she put her money to use in ways her father wouldn't have dreamed of, let alone actually done.

She thought of several of her overseas projects for orphaned children and swallowed the ache in her throat. 'Things change, Liam.'

'And some things stay the same,' he rejoined quietly.

Nikki rode out his innuendo with a small lift of her shoulders, finding it hard to believe how swiftly things between them had broken down again. Since the meningococcal scare, they seemed to have gone on a series of emotional highs and lows. Right now they were on another low, their relationship on the road to nowhere. She brought her head up, her voice holding the faintest thread of bitterness as she asked, 'Did you need me for something in particular or was this just an unfriendly visit?'

He chose to ignore the barbed little rider. 'I just wanted to let you know our flying pastor, Fergal Kennedy, is in town. He gets to Wirilda only occasionally so it's a bit of a break in routine for everyone.'

'I…see.' She didn't, but Liam was bound to offer more information if she waited long enough.

'He's here for a couple of days. Conducts a service at St Joseph's, does the rounds at the school, attends to any baptisms, counselling, that kind of thing, before he's off again.'

'So he's a kind of mission priest?'

Liam looked up sharply with a frown. 'Broadly speaking, yes. I suppose he is. Fergal's a great guy,' he added for good measure.

'So where do I come in?'

Liam's jaw clenched and he noticed the way her gaze fluttered down, as if just conversing with him made her switch off. Sweet God! How did he fix things? Every time he made up his mind to tell her how he felt, his tongue suddenly grew lead weights. 'I've offered him a bed for the two nights he's in town. The pub's pretty awful. Dion usually provides the hospitality but her kids have finished exams and are home early from boarding school so it's a bit of a crowd at their place.' A muscle in his jaw jerked as he drew to a stop.

'So are you seeking my approval?' she huffed through a jagged little laugh. 'It's your house, Liam. You can invite whomever you like to stay. Even an ex-wife…'

Liam's emotions began to show. 'I was merely doing you the courtesy of advising you of my plans to invite Fergal.'

'That's fine with me.' She stopped, too wearied with the effort of trying to keep her head straight around him.

'It won't be a problem, Nikki.' Liam got awkwardly to his feet. 'Fergal doesn't stand on ceremony. In fact, he'll probably offer to cook dinner. He's a great guy.'

'So you said.'

For a moment, Liam hovered uncertainly. 'I'll see you at home, then.' He turned abruptly, almost colliding with Grace as she burst in.

'Oh, good! You're both here. Urgent call from Lesley Manderson at the bakery.'

'What's up?' Liam said tersely.

Grace took a breath. 'Terry's grandad, Tom, is staying with them at the moment. He's gone fiddling with machinery and cut himself rather badly. Lesley's in a bit of a panic. She said there's blood all over the place and Terry's gone out somewhere.'

'Right.' Liam looked a question at Nikki. 'Like to come? Lesley might need a calming influence.'

'I'll grab my bag.' All antipathy forgotten, Nikki whirled to her feet. 'Meet you out front. And bring oxygen!' she called to Liam's back as he sped out of her room with Grace following.

Grace had almost to run to keep up with him. 'Should I call an ambulance?'

'Yes, please. Best to be on the safe side. I'd like back-up there in case we have to get him to the hospital.'

'Will do. And Lesley said they've closed for the day so could you go round the back?'

The bakery was barely half a block down the street so, rather than waste time getting in and out of Liam's car, they covered the distance on foot.

'Oh—thank you both for coming.' Lesley Manderson was on the lookout for them.

'Where is he?' Liam swept past her into the shop.

'Straight through to the little annexe.' She was all but wringing her hands. 'Tom was trying to fix the old bread-slicer. Those blades are lethal.' She winced. 'He's cut between his thumb and forefinger. He's not supposed to be in here at all!' she added emotionally. 'Terry's told him often enough.'

They found the old gentleman on the floor, his back braced against the wall, his hand wrapped tightly in a towel he was holding to his chest. He was very pale and obviously in shock. 'Bit of a mess…' he said weakly, as Liam hunkered down beside him.

Nikki turned urgently to Lesley Manderson. 'Is Tom on any medication?'

'Yes.' Lesley pressed her hand to her forehead. 'He had a slight stroke a few years ago. War-something.'

'Warfarin?' Nikki snapped her gaze to Liam's, and saw his mouth pull tight. That was all they needed. The drug was an anticlotting agent. She put her case down and snapped open the locks. They'd need a constriction bandage for the wound. And they'd better work fast.

'It's all right, Mr Manderson.' Liam was reassuring. 'I'm just going to pop this oxygen mask on you. It'll make you more comfortable. Breathe away now. Good man. Now, let's see what you've done to your hand, shall we?'

As Liam released the pressure on the wound, the blood spurted but he managed to staunch the bleeding just long enough to assess its severity. He frowned. It was jagged and nasty and if he wasn't mistaken, there was deep nerve and tissue damage. 'Let's get some pressure on this, please, Nikki.'

'Will Tom be all right?' Lesley hovered tearfully. 'Can I help?'

Nikki began applying the compression bandage to the wound. 'We need to get Tom's arm elevated, Lesley.' She spoke kindly. 'Think you could get something to make a sling?'

'I could rip up an old sheet.' The young woman

looked glad to be doing something. 'Won't be a tick. We live over the shop.'

'I'll give him a jab of morphine.' Liam selected the drug from Nikki's bag. In seconds he'd drawn up the dose. 'Poor old chap,' he murmured, adding ten milligrams of anti-emetic to help settle their patient's stomach.

'We should get some fluids into him, Liam.' Nikki was concerned about the tell-tale moistness of Tom Manderson's skin.

'Right. Get a line in if you can. I'll get a BP reading.'

Nikki worked quickly. It took precious time to tap a vein to the surface but finally she succeeded. 'OK, line's in and holding,' she breathed with relief, attaching it to the bag of saline. 'What's the BP?'

Liam frowned. 'Eighty-five on fifty-five. We need Haemaccel. Where the heck is the ambulance?'

They both knew the elderly man's position could become critical very quickly if he didn't receive the benefit of a plasma-expander.

'I did the best I could.' Lesley hurtled through the door. 'Will this do?' She held up the torn piece of sheeting.

'That's fine.' Expertly, Nikki folded the material to a manageable size to accommodate Tom's arm. Securing the sling gently, she tied the ends around his shoulder.

Wordlessly, Lesley shook her head. 'He looks so…frail.'

Liam took the young woman aside. 'He's very shocked, Lesley. We need to get him to hospital. Any chance you could get hold of Terry?'

'He should be here any minute.' Her gaze swung back to Tom. 'Is he—? He's not going to—?' She broke off, too overcome to speak, and pressed her hand to her throat. 'Oh!' She spun round with relief. 'Here's Terry now. And the ambulance!'

Terry Manderson was visibly shaken. 'I didn't believe it when the ambulance stopped here.' He reached out a hand to his wife. 'What's happened?'

'It's Tom!' She grabbed her husband's fingers and hung on. 'He's cut himself on the bread-slicer.'

'Oh, hell! Silly old coot! Where is he?'

'Calm down, Terry.' Liam was firm. 'Let Dr Barrett and the ambulance crew take care of your grandfather now. We need to get him to hospital.'

Terry swallowed and heaved in a controlling breath. 'Sorry. Yeah, OK. We'll follow the ambulance.'

Nikki had hooked up a line and begun running the blood product the ambulance had brought. So far, so good, she thought. But it was obvious Grandad Manderson was in for a long haul.

'OK, matey, let's go.' The ambulance crew lifted the stretcher and began easing it through the narrow doorway. 'You coming, Liam?'

'Be with you in two minutes.' Liam flicked a hand backwards.

'He's going to need microsurgery, isn't he?' Nikki began packing up her case.

'Yes.' Liam's voice was clipped. 'And an anaesthetic at his advanced age won't make it a walk in the park either.'

'You'll medivac him out?'

'What else can I do?' Liam swore under his breath,

clamping his hands to the sides of his head. 'I wish I had more skills!'

'For heaven's sake, don't start beating yourself up,' Nikki reproved softly. 'You do the work of ten doctors already.'

His smile was grim but at least it was there. 'It's good to have you in my corner, Nik.'

He'd actually noticed? Nikki lifted her eyes briefly to the ceiling then followed him out. 'It'll be all right. Tom has family. And from what little I observed, they love him to bits, even if he drives them to drink sometimes.'

Liam sent her a cock-eyed grin. 'Well, that covers most of us, doesn't it?'

CHAPTER TEN

NIKKI made her way slowly back to the surgery. Grace had locked up securely and gone home. Nikki thought she'd do the same. And she had yet to meet this friend of Liam's who was staying with them.

She sighed as she revved the Jeep and reversed out of the carport. Somehow she'd have to drag out her social skills for the evening when all she felt like doing was to have a shower and crawl into bed.

Fergal Kennedy was in the courtyard, admiring her herb spiral, when Nikki arrived home. She blinked. He was nothing like she'd imagined: tall and thin with a noticeably calm face and his fairish hair so thoroughly mixed with grey, it looked as though someone had swirled it about with a paintbrush. He was very informally dressed in jeans and an open-necked shirt.

'Hello.' His smile showed straight white teeth. 'You must be Nikki.' He held out his hand in greeting. 'I've made myself at home. I hope that's all right?'

'Of course it is.' Nikki warmed to him at once. 'It's nice to meet you, Reverend.'

'Oh, no!' Fergal spun a desperate look over his shoulder. 'He's not here, too, is he?'

Nikki chuckled. 'Fergal it is, then. Are you admiring my herbs?'

'Mmm. Did something like this myself once. They

never looked as good as yours, though.' They walked companionably up the steps to the deck. Fergal sent her a brief smile. 'Where's that man of yours? I've his favourite beer on ice.'

Nikki's heart gave a little flutter. 'Emergency call. He's at the hospital.' She put her case down and ran her hand across the back of her neck, absently finger-combing the short strands of hair at her nape. 'And Liam's not my man, Fergal.'

'Ah!' Fergal gave her a shrewd look, bracing his hands on the back of one of the outdoor chairs. 'I would've thought very differently, Nikki. But, then…' he spread his hands philosophically '…what do I know about anything?'

'Quite a lot, *I* would've thought.' Nikki's dry little smile activated the dimple in her cheek. 'Now, I'm going to excuse myself for a few minutes and have a shower. Keep making yourself at home. I won't be long.'

It was almost an hour later when Liam got home. By then Nikki had liberally sampled the fine wine Fergal had brought and, as the captive audience for his endless supply of silly jokes, she'd managed to cheer up. Now they were in the kitchen, bickering gently over the preparations for dinner.

'Our food's on the way, I see.' Parked against the doorframe, Liam looked on amusedly.

'Oh!' Nikki spun round and looked at him, her eyes over-bright. 'Hello, Liam.'

His mouth pleated in an uncertain smile. 'Hello, Nikki.'

'We're having pepper steaks and Fergal's warm ham salad,' she told him knowledgably.

'Warm *yam* salad!' Fergal mock-swiped her with the kitchen sponge. 'Sweet potatoes when they're at home.'

'Oops!' Nikki placed the tips of her fingers over her lips. 'Silly me.'

Fergal's grin was indulgent as he ground a final spray of pepper over the steaks and placed them under the grill. 'I expect you could kill for one of these, mate.' Opening the fridge door, he hauled out a couple of ice-cold lagers and passed one to Liam. 'Nikki said you had an emergency.'

Liam relaxed against the bench top and related the story of Tom Manderson's accident.

'Poor old chap.' Fergal ripped the top off his beer and took a mouthful. 'Where did you send him?'

'Actually, we were pretty lucky there.' Liam lifted a hand and rubbed the back of his neck. 'Sending Tom through to Brisbane would have meant an enormous upset for the whole family but it so happened the surgeon attached to the Flying Doctor Service was operating in Longreach today. He agreed to stay over and do Tom first thing in the morning.'

'Excellent.' Fergal nodded. 'Problem solved for everyone it would seem.'

'A much better outcome,' Nikki agreed quietly.

'You guys realise it's only a bit over five weeks until Christmas?' Fergal posed the question as he refilled the kettle and put it back on the gas to boil for their third pot of tea.

Nikki glanced at her watch, surprised to see it was almost midnight. At this rate they'd be talking the night away. But she hadn't enjoyed herself so much in ages. Fergal Kennedy was much travelled and such an interesting person. No wonder the locals looked forward to his visits.

'I wasn't actually counting.' Liam's mouth turned down. 'Not much Christmas spirit about with the drought lasting so long.'

'All the more reason we should think of ways to make it a Christmas the town will remember.' Fergal filled the teapot and brought it across to the table. 'Dion wants to form a committee to organise something. She'd like both you on board.'

'Do you plan to be here?' Liam passed his mug across for a refill.

'You bet.' Fergal took his time pouring the tea. 'All going well, I plan to arrive on Christmas Eve. I'll look forward to seeing you both.'

Nikki swallowed some of her tea. 'I mightn't be here,' she hedged. 'But I think it's a lovely idea, Fergal—to do something special for the local community. Do you have something in mind? You probably do—you've been in lots of places, under lots of different circumstances...' She drew to an awkward stop.

'Actually, Nikki, I thought *you* might.' Deftly, Fergal filled the uncomfortable silence that followed. 'Your experience with MSF should have turned up a few possibilities, surely?'

Her gaze faltered. 'I'll...give it some thought. Perhaps we can talk about it tomorrow...'

'I think it's tomorrow already.' Fergal raised his arms to half-mast and stretched, then pulled himself upright. 'I'm away to my bed, folks, so I'll wish you both goodnight.'

'Goodnight,' they echoed.

After Fergal had gone, there seemed a breathlessness in the air, a silence that was almost painful. Then, almost too calmly, Liam asked, 'What did you mean, you might not be here at Christmas?'

Nikki swallowed uncomfortably. 'My contract finishes early in December.'

Liam's heart began beating like a tom-tom. Had he hesitated too long? Found her only to lose her again? 'So what are you saying, Nikki?'

'You said we'd see what shape we were in after three months, Liam.' Her voice had lowered and tightened. 'And, frankly, I don't think we're in very good shape at all.'

'How can you say that?'

He sent her a smouldering look and she pressed her lips together, fighting off the avalanche of emotions at the recollection of those frenzied minutes in each other's arms so recently.

'I thought we were doing pretty well...' After a pause, he went on, 'Your involvement with the practice has meant the world to me. And I thought sharing a home was adding another dimension.'

Nikki gave a humourless little laugh. 'Co-existing but not really connecting.'

Liam ground out a harsh expletive. 'Do you think I haven't wanted to?'

'Then why haven't you, Liam? Heaven knows, you could have found an opportunity if you'd really wanted to.' Nikki's heart was pounding, and she could hardly breathe.

'There's no easy answer to that, Nikki.'

'For heaven's sake! I'm not hanging out for another marriage certificate. But I wanted us to be part of one another's lives again. In every way that counts. And if that's too far or too fast for you, then perhaps we'd better finish things. Perhaps I shouldn't even wait around until the three months are up…'

Liam felt the tightening in his throat. So tight he could barely swallow. 'Is this an ultimatum, Nikki?' His question was harshly muted. 'Either we become lovers again or you're out of here? Hell…' He pressed his fingers across his eyes in a weary gesture. 'Why don't you just put me up against the wall and shoot me for not performing?'

'Now who's being childish?' Nikki could feel her control slipping by the second. Suddenly she had the strong impression of the two of them floating away, like passengers in separate trains, side by side with no meeting point. 'Perhaps the notion to come here was a fantasy on my part. After all, it's not as though *you* kept in touch.'

Liam scrubbed a hand across his eyes. 'Nikki, this is doing my head in. I can't think any more. Just know I need you here.'

She gave a bitter laugh and got to her feet. 'You don't need me, Liam. You need my medical skills. But I care about the people here, so I'll stay until Christmas, help out where I can. After that…'

His jaw tightened. But he let her go without further comment.

A week later, Jade Murphy called at the surgery to see Nikki.

'Come in, Jade.' Nikki was a little surprised to see

her. 'If it's about the result of your pap smear, there's no problem.'

'That's good.' Jade seemed to have trouble dredging up a smile. 'I know I said I'd phone for the result, Nikki, but I wanted to talk to you in person.'

'Was there something else?' Nikki waved her to a chair. 'Something we didn't cover last time?'

Jade made a small face. 'Indirectly. But I wanted to tell you in person that I won't be showing up for any of the blood tests and so on.'

Nikki made a steeple of her fingers and propped them under her chin. It was obvious that whatever Jade had come about it was troubling her deeply.

'About having a baby…' Jade's mouth trembled slightly. 'Damien doesn't want us to go ahead and try.'

'And you're terribly disappointed,' Nikki said gently.

'Yes.' Jade blinked several times. 'Damien's excuse is that my job is so uncertain just now. He wants to wait until things come good again, until our financial future is secure. But that mightn't happen for ages.'

'Jade, you're only twenty-eight,' Nikki pointed out practically. 'You've oceans of time.'

'I know all that.' She shook her head. 'It was really Damien's attitude that threw me. He was just so inflexible—as though it was his decision and nothing to do with me…'

Jade's shoulders sagged and suddenly, without warning, she burst into tears. Nikki let her cry, then when she sniffed and hauled in a huge controlling breath, Nikki pushed a box of tissues towards her.

'Thanks…' Jade's voice was muffled as she mopped up. 'You think you know someone and then you find out you really don't know them at all.'

Well, she could identify with that, Nikki silently agreed. But Jade was the patient here and it was clear she and her husband were terribly out of sync. And where they should have been on a high about the possibility of starting a family, because of circumstances beyond their control, their hopes had been dashed.

'Perhaps it was a knee-jerk reaction from Damien.' Nikki sought to rationalise the situation. 'Because of the drought, many of the menfolk are suddenly finding themselves vulnerable, their feelings of self-worth crushed when they see themselves as unable to provide properly for their families. Perhaps Damien is being influenced by what he sees amongst his male workmates and friends.'

Jade sighed and shook her head. 'Do you think it could be as simple as that? That he's in some kind of panic mode?'

Nikki lifted a shoulder. 'It's a powerful emotion. And then self-doubt starts creeping in. And having a baby, as you said yourself, is a huge responsibility.'

'We depend on my job quite a lot.' Jade began to slowly make sense of things. 'It's not like in our grandmother's day when the woman's role was solely that of a home-maker.' She managed a watery smile. 'Although that would drive me nuts, I think.'

'They were the social mores of the time, I guess.' Nikki spread her hands in a shrug. 'But it would be lovely if women actually had the choice to work or not.'

'But not a real world,' Jade came back wryly. 'Thanks for letting me talk this through, Nikki.' She gave an upside-down smile. 'I probably made a mountain out of a molehill. I think I can understand where Damien is coming from now. He's all stiff and uncommunicative presently but I know of a way to thaw him out.' She blushed prettily. 'And who knows?' She got to her feet. 'Perhaps the school will recoup the funding and my job will be safe again.'

As she said goodbye to Jade, Nikki turned to see Liam just coming out of his consulting room. He had a small, dark-haired woman with him and it was obvious she'd been crying. It must be the day for it, Nikki thought sadly, and slipped quietly back to her own room.

Several minutes later Liam rapped and came in. 'Grace said you'd finished and I'd like a word, please.'

'Well, that makes a change.'

He stared at her in silence for a moment, his jaw clenched, a muscle jumping. 'Look, can we call a truce?' he asked without preamble. 'Things are difficult enough without this kind of cold war that seems to have sprung out of nowhere.'

Nikki bristled. For the past week he'd avoided her whenever possible, being scrupulously polite but remote whenever they'd been forced to interact. 'You chose to crawl back into your shell, Liam,' she challenged him.

His mouth twisted in the parody of a smile. 'What kind of shell are we talking about here? Clam, tortoise, crab? I doubt I'd fit in any of those.'

Just the mental picture he'd created made her

smile reluctantly. 'OK...' She exhaled a long breath. 'Truce.' She waved him to a chair. 'What's up?'

'We have our first case of drought-related domestic violence.'

'Oh, lord.' Nikki looked appalled. 'The little woman you were seeing out earlier?'

'Yes.' His mouth compressed for a second. 'Leila Drummond. And it's the same old story—argument over money. Her husband lost his job some time back, self-esteem down the gurgler. Leila had given him the responsibility of buying something for the kids' tea.' Liam lifted his hands in a Gallic shrug. 'He detoured to the pub.'

'Brilliant. What's the damage to Mrs Drummond?'

'Bruising to her ribs. She said it was one wild swipe in frustration and she got in the way of it. Barry had never done anything like that before.'

Nikki's eyebrows rose. 'Do you believe that?'

'I've no reason not to.' Liam's mouth twisted into a thoughtful moue. 'I've had a few dealings with Barry Drummond and he's seemed an OK guy. But obviously they won't want any of this to leak out. In a small community like ours, facts can rapidly become distorted and Barry could be labelled a wife-beater. The result would be horrendous for the whole family. Leila only came to me because she needed a certificate for work. She can barely lift her arm on the injured side.'

Nikki winced. 'I don't imagine she came right out and said her husband had struck her—accidentally or not.'

'Said she fell.' Liam rubbed behind his neck wearily. 'She crumpled when I began asking for more details. And then the whole sorry tale came out.'

'Hmm.' Nikki looked thoughtful. Picking up her pen, she spun it back and forth between her fingers. 'So, as medical officers, what practical help can we offer this family?'

Liam looked taken aback.

'Come on, Liam, think!' Nikki swung off her chair and went to the window, tapping her fingertips on the sill and looking out. Suddenly she turned. 'What kind of work does Leila do?'

'Ah, cleaner at the hospital.'

'And I presume Barry will know *you* know about his misdemeanour?'

'He drove Leila to the surgery, so I imagine so. Just what are you getting at here, Nikki?' Liam studied his fingertips for a moment and then brought his gaze up in query. 'That he'll want to prove it was a one-off and won't happen again?'

'Something like that. So why don't we think creatively here? The hospital is going to be a cleaner down until Leila is fit for work. What's to stop Barry getting his butt over there and offering to substitute?'

Liam sat back, stunned. 'Nothing, I suppose. I'd have to have a confidential word with Anna—and she'd have to be prepared to take him on. But as long as Barry was prepared to do it...'

Nikki dimpled. 'I'm sure you could liaise beautifully, Dr Donovan.'

'Could I just?' Liam flashed a dry grin across at her. 'Why don't we go the whole hog and suggest the Drummonds job-share?'

'Oh, my goodness!' Nikki stopped as if struck.

'That's a brilliant idea! And it could work. Instead of collecting the dole, Barry would be back in the paid workforce, feeling useful, and Leila would be less pressured and able to have more time for herself and the children.'

'And they all lived happily ever after.' Liam got to his feet and pushed his chair in, his fingers curled across the back. He shook his head. 'You're still the most outrageous fixer-upper I know.'

Was that a compliment or not? She blinked at him and for a split second the world seemed to telescope. And then he was holding out his arms, wide and welcoming.

Nikki's feet suddenly had wings.

Liam's arms wrapped round her, strong and tender. One large hand cradled the back of her head as he held her, rocking her like a child.

Nikki felt her body relax against him. It felt so absolutely right to be holding one another like this. After the longest time she drew back, looking at him. 'I hate it when we're not friends.' The words trembled on her lips. 'Is there still a chance for us, Liam?'

'I don't deserve you…' His words were muffled against her hair. 'We'll work something out, Nik. Somehow.'

Reaching up, she smoothed the dark hair away from his forehead, ran her fingers over his temples, the outer edges of his ears. She could only hope he was right.

Her phone rang and she half turned towards the sound. 'Go and see Anna.' She gave him a urgent nudge towards the door.

'And then I suppose you want me to go and see the Drummonds?' His smile was decidedly wry.

'If Anna's onside, yes. We have the chance to change things for this family, Liam. Leila and Barry are probably sitting at home, feeling as miserable as sin. Now, go, while I see who's on the other end of this call.'

Nikki's caller was Dion Westermann. 'I haven't had much luck at all in getting a committee together for our Christmas project,' the council alderman confessed ruefully.

'Liam and I will be glad to help, Dion.' Nikki made a face at the opposite wall and wondered if she was arbitrarily volunteering Liam's services. But he'd want to be involved, surely?

'Well, that makes four of us,' Dion said. 'I've got Anna Marshall to come on board, although reluctantly. She has such a lot on her plate, like all health professionals.'

Nikki was hastily tapping into every one of her organisational skills. 'Dion, four is more than enough for a steering committee. What we need are a willing band of auxiliary helpers to carry out the plans for the day. I have several people in mind.'

'Nikki, you're a marvel.' Dion sounded relieved. 'And I'll volunteer my two teenagers.' She cackled. 'They're quite used to taking direction. Now, as for the celebration itself, I thought of one huge party on Christmas Eve in the hall, together with a giant Christmas tree—if we can find one that hasn't gone under in the drought.' She gave a hollow laugh.

'We'll find one.' Nikki wasn't about to give in to any negative possibilities. 'And most families have a box of decorations tucked away at home, don't they? So, if everyone contributed a few of their own bits and pieces, the tree could be decorated without any money having to be spent.'

'And it's another way of involving the community,' Dion agreed.

'And I think it's essential we provide a small gift for everyone, Dion.' Nikki grabbed a pen and scribble pad.

'That could prove quite expensive.' Dion sounded a note of caution. 'And what about the food? Do we ask people to bring something? But then that could turn out a bit of a mish-mash. And the women would have to spend precious time baking…'

Nikki doodled on her pad. 'You think providing a traditional Christmas dinner with all the trimmings is the way to go, then?'

'Ideally, yes. Then it would be a real treat for everyone just to come along and partake.'

'In that case, we'd need caterers.'

'Mmm. So we should open some kind of Christmas fund.' Dion considered carefully. 'I realise there's not much money around but if we can whip up enough community spirit, my guess is folk will find a dollar here and there. I'll kick it off with a substantial donation from the council,' the alderman promised.

'Then I'll match it, personally.' Nikki was on a roll. 'And, Dion, I'm sure I don't need to tell you I'd like anonymity about this.'

'You have my word, Nikki. But are you sure? I mean, I don't know what kind of funding the mayor will release. It could be, well, substantial.'

Nikki gave a weak laugh. 'I hope it will be. And not to worry. I had a bit of a windfall on the stock market recently and I can't think of a better use for the money.' And it might be the last thing she could do for Wirilda and its people if she had to leave...

Later that day, Nikki looked up from preparing dinner as Liam came through the kitchen door. 'So, how did you get on?'

'Pretty good, actually.' He threw himself into a chair and wrenched open a couple of buttons on his shirt. 'Anna was a pushover. Leila is one of her best workers.'

'Excellent.' Nikki moved to the stove, turning the meat under the grill, deciding ruefully that she was almost looking like a chop herself these days. But there was precious little chance of varying their diet. It seemed the local butcher, along with the rest of the shopkeepers, had all but lost heart in his business.

She began to strip the leaves off some stalks of mint, thanking heaven for their little herb patch. At least some of their meals could be spiced up a bit. 'And the Drummonds?' she asked pointedly.

Liam rocked his hand. 'Took a bit of persuading but Barry has agreed to go and see Anna at the hospital this evening. She's on a late.'

Nikki rolled the mint leaves and began chopping them roughly. 'Did you mention the idea of job-sharing to Anna?'

'I did.' Liam spun his hands up behind his neck. 'She was intrigued, to say the least.' His mouth flickered in a smile. 'She'll see how Barry shapes up. If he shows enthusiasm, there's a chance he could be made permanent but in a job of his own.'

Nikki blinked. 'My goodness. How did that come about?'

'Anna said they've just received a special grant for hospitals in drought-affected areas,' he explained. 'Apparently, the place urgently needs a maintenance person but they haven't been able to afford one. And Barry, when he can get work, is a builder's labourer.'

Nikki's face was wreathed in smiles. 'So he'll know his way around a toolbox, won't he? Oh, I hope it works out!'

Liam's look was droll. 'Well, *we've* given it our best shot at any rate.'

'Sometimes it's just timing,' Nikki dismissed airily.

'With a great big shove in the right direction from certain people.' Liam glanced meaningfully at her and pushed himself upright. 'You seem to have dinner under control, so I'll grab a shower.' He flicked the hair at her nape, as he passed. 'I'll cook tomorrow.'

'Ah, about tomorrow…'

Immediately Liam was alerted by her uneasy little laugh.

'Why do I get the feeling I'm being set up again?'

'Would I do that?' She sent him a wounded look.

'Go on.' His look was indulgent as he pretended to be considering the implications.

'Well…' Nikki turned down the grill and gave him her full attention. 'I thought we could take a picnic down by the river.'

'You mean what's left of the river.' Liam helped

himself to a curl of lettuce from the salad bowl. 'And why are we doing that? Or shouldn't I ask?'

Nikki slapped his hand as he dipped into the bowl again. 'I want to check out the possibility of finding a Christmas tree. We're going to need a huge one for our party at the hall on Christmas Eve.'

'And when was all this decided?'

'Dion called me this afternoon.'

'OK.' Liam held up his hands in mock surrender. 'Tell me the rest over dinner.'

'Oh, Liam?' Nikki called cheekily when he was about to disappear out the door. 'I volunteered you for the steering committee.'

Hand on the doorframe, Liam kept his gaze averted, an intensity of emotion he'd never felt before gnawing at his insides. This was his Nikki in full beautiful flight, the Nikki he knew and…loved. He closed his eyes and gave a silent, hollow laugh. And *love* was the word he'd been avoiding all this time.

But it was still there like a bright light leading him home.

Suddenly his heartbeat was deafening. He'd waffled on about want and need. But never about love. His eyes clouded and there was a lump in his throat the size of a lemon. Did he have time to put things right? Did he still have a chance—or had Nikki already given up on him?

CHAPTER ELEVEN

NEXT afternoon they took their picnic, some vegetable parcels made with puff pastry Nikki was keeping warm in aluminium foil, and settled themselves in some shade along the river bank.

'These are good.' Liam bit into the crisp pastry hungrily.

'They're from the bakery.' Nikki smiled. 'Grace's idea.'

'Sure beats last night's chops. Hey, I'm not blaming the cook!' Liam dodged the wrapper she threw at him.

Nikki gave a reluctant chuckle. 'They were as tough as toenails, weren't they?'

Liam shuddered. 'Perhaps that's what we were eating—old toenails.'

'By the time I'd got to the butcher's, there was practically nothing left,' Nikki lamented. 'All the shops look so weary, Liam.'

'And their owners.'

Nikki filled their mugs with tea from a flask. 'When will it rain?'

'They've had good falls on the coast.' Liam took a careful mouthful of his tea. 'Perhaps it will make its way to us soon.'

But would it be soon enough? Nikki put up a hand and swatted another intrusive bush fly.

'So, where are we looking for this Christmas tree?'

Liam asked after a while, emptying the dregs of his tea onto the ground.

Nikki clicked her tongue. 'I thought you'd know.' They bent together to gather up the fragments from their picnic.

'I asked around a bit today,' he confessed sheepishly. 'We're on the lookout for a pine tree. Apparently they're extremely hardy.'

'But around here?' Nikki's frown reflected her doubt.

Liam shoved their rubbish into a plastic bag and tied it up. 'Well, according to this Aboriginal old-timer I asked, there used to be a pine plantation around Wirilda.'

Nikki snorted. 'When, a hundred years ago?'

'Possibly.' Liam knuckled her cheek playfully. 'But the seeds can be carried, either by birds or flooding rain, and they can germinate and end up anywhere.'

'So we could possibly find one, then?' Her face was suddenly a study in bright anticipation.

'It's quite likely.' Raising his face to the sky, Liam gauged how much daylight was left. 'Right, we'd better get cracking.' He held out his hand. 'Ready?'

'Yes.' Nikki was almost dizzy with the touch of his skin on hers, the grip of his lean powerful fingers, the absolute rightness of her hand in his, as they set off.

They walked along, sometimes breaking the companionable silence to talk casually. To the west, the rich bold colours of the sunset had all but faded, leaving the promise of a night sky so clear, it looked almost opaque.

Nikki looked around her, taking in the remoteness and the silence as they changed direction and headed up along a track sprinkled with boulders. A strange unease began to nibble at the edges of her mind and she tugged Liam to a stop. 'We seem to have come miles. We're not lost, are we?'

'And you a former Guide!' There was a teasing glint in Liam's eyes. 'Except for this detour, we've merely been following the line of the river. When we find our tree, we'll just turn around and return the way we've come.'

'You seem certain we'll find this elusive pine tree.'

Liam took her gently by the shoulders. 'Cubby Daylight is one of the tribal elders. He knows this place like the back of his hand. His people used to hunt and gather here. And if he says there's a pine tree, then there's a pine tree.'

Nikki still looked unconvinced. She had visions of them walking in circles until it got dark. 'I'd feel happier if I knew where we were aiming for, Liam.'

Liam clicked his tongue. 'Come on, Nik. Don't be a wimp. Cubby gave me a fair idea where to look. And I'd say we're almost there. Look up.' There was a note of triumph in his voice as he pointed to where a rocky overhang jutted out like a protecting umbrella.

Nikki tipped her head back, her gaze travelling up the craggy outcrop, past a spindly stringy bark tree, on past the spiny-leaved tussocks to the top. 'Oh, Liam…' Her voice was hushed in unbelief. There, right at the top, was not one but a small battalion of the most amazing pine trees. Dark green and uniformly beautiful. 'Yes!' She turned to him, her laugh ringing out, turning to a shriek as Liam picked her up and whirled her in a little circle, then gathered her in.

'Think you'll find one to suit amongst that lot?' His question was muted, his eyes on her flushed face with the intensity of a camera lens.

'Oh, yes.' Her eyes were shining. 'That one on the end, see?' She pointed.

'It must be nearly fifteen feet high.'

'Won't it look splendid all decorated?'

'Am I being roped in for that as well?' He touched her hair, his hand lingering over its dark silkiness.

'No.' Nikki rested her head against his chest, feeling the solid beat of his heart. 'I have that organised.'

'I'll just bet you do,' he murmured, bending to kiss her, taking his time over it, until she parted her lips.

On a little whimper Nikki burrowed closer, drinking him in, feeling the absorption of his scent in her nostrils, through her skin.

When they drew apart, they stared at one another, the moment almost surreal. Nikki was the first to break the silence with a tattered sigh. 'I'll always remember this moment, Liam—the moment we discovered our tree.'

The tip of his finger outlined her mouth. 'And perhaps we've discovered a bit more than just our tree.'

'Perhaps.' She snuggled closer.

The next day, Nikki telephoned Jade.

'I need your help with this Christmas party,' she explained.

'Doesn't it sound fabulous?' Jade's excitement was evident. 'The town is just buzzing. I'd be glad to lend a hand, Nikki. Just tell me what you'd like me to do.'

'Come to a meeting of the steering committee this evening for starters.' Nikki laughed. 'It'll be at Alderman Westermann's home at seven-thirty. Can you make it?'

It seemed Jade could.

'Things are moving along nicely,' Dion informed the little gathering in her lounge room that evening. 'Everyone's been beavering away behind the scenes and the whole evening promises to be something the town won't forget.'

'I've lined up the caterers from Brisbane,' Nikki said. 'They'll give us a cut rate and the menu looks wonderful. The only thing is, they'll need facilities here to prepare the food.'

'That won't be a problem.' Dion flapped a hand. 'The kitchen at the hall was modernised a couple of years ago when Wirilda had a teeming social life. Most functions were very successfully catered for there.'

'What about the tree itself?' Anna spoke for the first time.

Nikki's heart unaccountably thumped. 'Liam and I found a beauty up on the north ridge yesterday. Brett and some of the SES guys are going to arrange its removal. They've promised to have it set up in the hall in plenty of time for the decorating committee.'

'A decorating committee.' Jade snickered. 'Doesn't that sound grand? Are they going to have a theme?'

'Wouldn't think so.' Liam made a sound somewhere between a snort and a laugh. 'By the time everyone drapes a bit of their own stuff over the branches, I imagine we'll be looking at colourful rather than creative.'

There was laughter around the circle and then Jade said, 'Nikki, you mentioned wanting the schoolchildren's involvement in a special project?'

'Thank you, Jade. Yes.' Nikki swung her gaze to link the committee members. 'It's about providing gifts for everyone. I've this consignment of empty shoeboxes arriving on next week's plane.'

Jade chuckled. 'Well, that's original. Are we going to put something in them?'

Nikki grinned. 'I'm coming to that. The kids still have a couple of weeks before they break up for holidays and if it's the same as when I went to school, they're mostly at a loose end until then.'

'Tell me about it,' Jade said with a roll of her eyes. 'Exams are over and, as the teacher aide, I'm at my wit's end trying to think of things for them to do.'

'So we get them occupied covering the shoeboxes in nice bright Christmas wrapping,' Nikki explained. 'I've rolls of that coming as well, plus cartons of various goodies to put in the boxes. But the adults will do the filling part—secretly, of course. And on Christmas Eve each family will receive their own special Christmas box from under the tree.'

'That sounds lovely, Nikki. And very innovative.' Anna looked uncertain. 'But do we have that kind of money to spend?'

'The council came up with some funds.' Nikki waved a hand airily. 'And there were a few extra donations made…'

'Anonymously and substantially, one presumes,' Liam muttered under his breath, and Nikki coloured faintly.

'Well, I think it's absolutely perfect,' Jade came in supportively. 'And I think Nikki deserves a big vote of thanks.' She turned to Nikki with a question. 'But how have you been able to arrange it all so quickly?'

'Called in a few favours,' Nikki flannelled. And it helped to have a fistful of money at her disposal, she qualified silently. 'I still have contacts from my time with Médecins Sans Frontières.'

'Doctors Without Borders.' Dion looked impressed. 'Is that where this idea for the shoeboxes came from, then?'

'Basically. We did something similar when I was in North Vietnam but it was mainly for the orphaned children in an effort to make their Christmas a bit special.'

'Poor little mites,' Anna murmured.

'I recall one of the children especially...' Nikki bit her lip. 'A thirteen-year-old girl with a tiny baby. She'd been trapped in a refugee camp for years, had received almost no formal schooling. She'd never been given a gift in her entire life. Heck, what am I saying? None of those children had ever had as much as a lollypop given to them.'

There was a beat of silence.

'Oh, how sad.' Jade blinked back a sudden tear. 'I'll never complain again about my lot in life. In reality, we all have so much to be thankful for, don't we? And, Nikki, thank *you*. I feel so privileged to be able to help with your project. And despite the hardship in the town, I predict it's going to be a very special Christmas.'

'Hear, hear,' echoed softly around the gathering.

'Just one more thing before we close.' Dion held up a detaining hand. 'Perhaps we should avoid serving alcohol on the evening. We don't want any mishaps as folk make their way home. That would be too awful.'

Liam drew his legs up and sat back in his chair. 'I don't think one glass of champagne apiece would hurt, Dion. I'd be happy to donate it.'

Dion wavered and then made a throw-away motion with her hands. 'That's very generous of you, Liam. And who knows?' she added with a hopeful smile. 'Perhaps there'll be something else along with Christmas to celebrate.'

'Like rain!' Anna and Jade said together.

'You sly philanthropist, you.' Liam's voice mocked Nikki gently as they drove home from the meeting.

'And who's donating crates of champagne?' she countered spiritedly.

He laughed. 'Think your caterers could supply some decent stuff?'

Nikki's mouth curled into a prim little moue. 'I dare say it could be arranged. I'll need your cheque up-front, though, otherwise they'll stick me with the bill.'

'Your wish is my command, Dr Barrett.'

Nikki made a mock swipe at him, a shiver of awareness shafting through her when his hand reached out and imprisoned her fingers. He raised them gently to his lips. 'I'm so sorry, Nik...' His voice roughened. 'I've been an idiot, haven't I?'

Nikki gave a strangled laugh, blinking through a sudden lens of tears. 'Just marginally.'

'Do you feel terribly aggrieved?'

The swift overflow of tears unbalanced her, as had the starkness of his question. But she did feel aggrieved. He'd guessed that correctly.

Ever since she'd come to Wirilda, it seemed she'd done all the running, planned all the opportunities for something to happen between them. And his response had been to blow hot and then cold, to build a fence around his emotions and consign the tender buds of their possible reconciliation to the scrap heap.

Yet she'd always known he was by nature a cautious man. He'd had to be, he'd told her early on in their relationship. He had no wealthy father to bail him out if he made the wrong choices.

She heard him drag in a deep breath, then he spoke quietly. 'Over the past twenty-four hours I feel as though I've been hit with a rock from a great height.'

He sounded curiously vulnerable and Nikki's resentment faded.

She turned her head away, her voice cracking. 'Has it knocked some sense into you?'

There was an endless, breathless silence.

'Tell you when we get home,' he said eventually.

Nikki closed her eyes and hung on and in barely minutes they'd swept into his drive and jerked to a halt.

'That was some ride,' she said weakly.

He stabbed a hand through his hair. 'Sorry, there

are things I need to say to you.' He slid out and opened her door and they went inside. Alerted by their arrival, Lightning jumped down from his perch on the gatepost and followed them in.

Liam pushed the cat aside and turned awkwardly to Nikki. 'Give me your hands.'

She did and he began to chafe them briskly. 'Liam…' She caught hold of his wrists. 'I'm not cold.'

'No. Sorry. Uh, I don't know where to start.'

The ghost of a smile played around her lips and she became aware of the accelerated beat of her heart and a singing in her veins. 'Perhaps we could begin by holding each other.'

'Yes.' His eyes squeezed shut and when he opened them they were lit with purpose. 'I love you,' he said at last.

Nikki clamped hard on her bottom lip, watching as his face worked, his broad chest rise and fall in a broken sigh.

It was more than she could bear.

In a second they'd reached for one another, their bodies surging together like waves hell-bent on reaching the shore. Nikki could feel the jerky rhythm of his breathing, hear the rasp of it through the wall of her own emotions.

Like someone who had been away from home for a long, long time, she began re-exploring him, revelling in the whole of him, his familiarity. 'I love you, too…' She hadn't said it so openly, so honestly since the first time they'd made love.

Slowly she became aware of his palm resting gently against the nape of her neck while his fingers pushed up through the lowest strands of her hair, and she was aware of nothing but the sensation seeping through her body like the spread of a wonderful, delicious warmth.

'Oh, Nik…' His voice broke. 'I've been trying to come to terms with all these feelings I've had and all the while what I truly felt was staring me in the face.'

'And now?' she asked, her throat dry.

'Now?' His eyes were so close to hers she could see flecks of black in the brown. 'Now I want you with me always. If you'll have me…'

She felt the warm flood of desire ripple through her body. 'Of course I'll have you, you crazy man. Of course—'

Her words were blotted out by his kiss, and she responded with a wildness that matched his own, filled with a need to be part of him, to hold him and have him hold her. For ever.

Finally they pulled back, standing close, looking into each other's eyes. 'Don't ask me to sleep alone tonight.' Liam traced his lips along her throat, behind her ear, against her hair.

'The cat, mind the cat.' She stifled a giggle as Lightning purred and pressed around their ankles.

'What a passion-killer,' Liam muttered, hefting the animal gently with his shoe and shutting him outside.

Nikki extended a hand to him. 'Come,' she said softly.

His fingers tightened on hers. 'Come where?'

She laughed, the sound like music to his ears.

'To bed. It's OK.' She went on tiptoe and kissed him gently. 'We're allowed to.'

In the bedroom Liam's eyes clouded and he drew her close again. 'Are you sure about this, Nikki?'

'Need you ask?' She hugged him, tears filling her eyes.

He held her away from him, tracing down the outsides of her arms with his fingertips. 'I've dreamed of you like this. A thousand times.'

She swallowed and smiled and held his gaze. 'Shall we have a candle?'

She took his silence as a yes.

The candlelight was soft, giving off a shadowed beam across the pillows as they undressed without shame or shyness.

'I hardly dare believe this…' Liam brought her slowly against him. Lowering his head, he captured her mouth, his hands sliding intimately from her shoulders to her thighs.

'Are you real, my Nikki?'

'I'm real.' Her voice was so small she could hardly hear it herself. And nervous.

The floor shifted beneath her, then disappeared as he lifted her in his arms, drawing her down with him onto the bed. She shivered, wrapping her bare legs around him, her arms reaching up to pull his head down, sighing as she felt his warm weight against her skin.

'God, I've missed you,' he confirmed thickly, lowering his mouth to hers.

Nikki wanted him. Wanted everything to be wonderful. And it was. They fitted together perfectly as they'd always done.

She urged him closer and closer. Here was their meeting point, the renewal of their love at last.

She cried out, knowing he had found his place at the very centre of her being, where he should always have been and where he would now be for ever.

Blinded by tears of happiness, she pressed her face to his, her voice fracturing as she whispered, 'Promise you'll never leave me again.'

He buried his face in her tears and they mingled with his own. 'I promise.'

It was the day before Christmas Eve.

'I had a peek inside the hall today.' They'd finished their evening meal and were doing the washing-up.

At least Nikki was. Liam was looking at the calendar on the wall. 'Mmm. How was it?'

She chuckled. 'A hive of activity but starting to look very festive.'

'Oh, good,' he said absently. 'I figure if we can get locum cover, we should be able to take a couple of weeks off towards the end of January.'

Nikki turned and studied his back. 'Where would we go?'

'One of the Barrier Reef islands. I've already looked up some resort accommodation on the net. I found a place that looks promising.' His grin was faintly sheepish. 'It's got a suite with a circular bed.'

'Oh, my!' She laughed a husky feminine laugh that made his body clench. 'I've never tried one of those—have you?'

No.' His answering smile was as old as time. 'Shall I go ahead and book it, then? And hope like mad we can get a locum?'

'Let's,' she said softly, going to him.

Liam swept her up in his arms, hugging her hard against his chest, his head pressed close to hers. 'Let's throw our bread on the water. Is that what you're saying?'

She looked into his eyes, reading the sincerity in them, the love. 'It's worked for us so far, hasn't it?'

'Yes, it has,' he murmured unsteadily.

When the phone shrilled its summons, it took them several seconds to register the intrusive sound. 'Yours or mine?' Liam asked, his cheek against her hair.

She gave a throaty chuckle, twisting her head to look in his face. 'Definitely yours. But I'll come, too, if you need me.'

'Always.' He swiped a kiss across her nose and went to answer the call.

'It was the hospital,' he relayed economically. 'Michelle says they have an imminent birth. A young couple just turned up at the hospital. Mum looks a bit iffy, according to Michelle.'

'Let's go, then.' Nikki was already halfway to the door.

Michelle met them at the nurses' station. 'Oh, good, you've both come,' she said as if seeing them together was the norm.

'What can you tell us, Michelle?' Liam's voice was clipped.

'OK. Our couple are Aaron and Jody Morrison. They're very young and very scared. I managed to get Jody into the shower before I called you.' Michelle led the way along the short corridor to the midwifery suite. 'But then things started hotting up and I've put her straight into the delivery room.'

One look at their patient told both doctors Michelle's instincts had been right. This new life was not about to wait. Under Nikki's gentle questioning Jody revealed that her labour had progressed slowly and steadily all day.

'I'm looking for work.' Aaron Morrison held tightly to his wife's hand. 'We've been on the road since early this morning. And then Jody started feeling sick so we had to find a hospital fast.'

'Right.' Liam's tone was brisk. He turned to the young father-to-be. 'We'll need to examine Jody now, so if you'd step outside for a few minutes?'

'She's tiny, isn't she?' Nikki murmured as they scrubbed.

'Mmm.' Liam chewed his lip thoughtfully. 'Let's hope she's not in for a bumpy ride.'

Nikki sent him a quick discerning look. A Caesarean? Not if they could help it.

'Perhaps not.' Liam pulled on his gloves. Turning, he sent a reassuring smile to their patient. 'I'll be as gentle as I can, Jody,' he promised, beginning his internal examination.

Jody looked at him with huge, frightened eyes.

'She's fully dilated and the baby seems rather small.' Liam quietly gave his findings to Nikki. 'I'd be inclined to let her try to deliver naturally.'

'I'll proceed normally, then.' Nikki moved to cannulate Jody, taking the bag of saline Michelle had ready.

The fluids would keep the line open, saving them precious time in the event of an emergency when drugs would have to be injected in seconds.

Hooking up the drip, Nikki felt a surge of energy.

She was quietly confident they could deliver Jody of a healthy baby without difficulty.

But thirty minutes later she wasn't so sure. Each contraction seemed longer and more painful than the last, and Jody was becoming distressed.

Aaron's thin arms supported his wife's shoulders. 'This is killing her!' He looked wildly at the medical team. 'Can't you give her something?'

'No, Aaron, we can't.' Liam was firm. 'Jody's progressed too far into her labour. Any drugs now would cross the placenta and possibly harm your baby.'

'Come on now, Jody,' Nikki coaxed. 'You're doing so well. You're nearly there.'

'I can't do this,' she sobbed. 'Just…get the baby out—please…'

'How's her BP, Michelle?' Liam's face was set in harsh lines.

In a few seconds Michelle relayed the reading. 'One-sixty over seventy.'

Nikki pressed her lips together. The blood pressure was elevated but that was to be expected. Nevertheless, she felt a lick of unease. Had they done the right thing in even allowing this petite girl to try for a natural birth?

Now it seemed the only safe measure left to them was for Jody to use the nitrous oxide gas.

Quickly Nikki whipped the mask from its repository and instructed Jody how to use it, praying the gas would blur the pain and allow Jody to ride out the contractions.

'Heart rate one-eighty,' Michelle reported calmly.

'Come on, now, Jody…' Liam was cajoling. 'Here's a big one. Give me a push. Good girl. Go gently now. Don't strain. You're nearly there.' He spun to Michelle. 'Episiotomy tray ready?'

'Wait, Liam,' Nikki cut in urgently. 'She may not tear. Oh, look—she's managed beautifully!' Nikki's voice held pure relief as the baby's head crowned. 'Well done, Jody! You're a star!'

'You have a son,' Liam said, expertly clamping and cutting the cord a little later. In seconds he'd removed the infant to a nearby examination table.

One glance at the newborn's stillness, his blueness, told Nikki they had a problem. Her heart squeezed tight as she ran a stethoscope over the infant. 'We've got a heartbeat,' she said, tossing the stethoscope aside. 'I'll suction. Get ready to bag him, Liam. We're not about to lose this little man.'

Deftly, Liam placed the tiny Air Viva mask over the baby's nose and mouth, willing his own breath into the flat little lungs. And then, thankfully, they heard the most beautiful sound in the world, a splutter and a cough followed by an indignant little squawk.

Liam nodded, his mouth compressing. 'He'll make it.'

'Eureka…' Nikki felt her legs turn to jelly.

An hour later, with the baby checked over and Jody tidied up, the doctors were on their way home.

'The bub was tiny,' Nikki said. 'But I think he'll do quite well, don't you?'

'I've delivered smaller and they've thrived so, yes, baby Morrison will do nicely,' Liam agreed. 'But that young man has taken on quite a lot, hasn't he? No job and a new baby to look out for.'

'With so much Christmas spirit about, I'm sure

something will turn up.' Nikki's voice held a ring of confidence.

'And we'll keep mother and babe as long as we decently can. That will give Aaron some space to organise something.'

'You're really a very nice man, aren't you, Dr Donovan?' Nikki's hand went across to rest on his thigh.

'*We* haven't talked about having babies.' Liam placed his hand over hers and squeezed.

'I'd like some, wouldn't you?' In the dimness of the car, Nikki spun him a soft look.

'It would be the most wonderful gift to have a child with you, Nikki,' Liam said gruffly.

For answer, she turned her hand over and returned the pressure on his fingers as emotion swamped her. 'I imagine Clare would adore to be someone's nan… Even my father would probably like the idea of a grandchild.'

Liam frowned. 'Are you in touch with him?'

'Yes.' It was a mere breath of sound. 'He knows I'm here with you.'

Liam snorted. 'And?'

'And nothing. He's mellowed, Liam. He really has.'

'Does he still hate my guts?'

'These days he doesn't hate anyone's guts,' she reproved. 'He had a cancer scare a couple of years ago. That rather showed him that money couldn't buy him immediate good health.'

Liam softened slightly. 'How is he now?'

'No recurrence so far.' She huffed a wry laugh. 'And at least it made him give up smoking.'

They were quiet for a while, locked in their own private thoughts.

'Excited about tomorrow?' Liam brought her knuckles to his lips.

Excited didn't begin to describe it. She curled herself against him as far as the seat belt would allow. 'We're having only a morning surgery,' she reminded him.

'Will that give you enough time?'

'I'll have heaps. The whole community has been on a roll. There's hardly been anything for me to do.' In fact, Nikki had been stunned by the endless goodwill the people of Wirilda continued to show towards her. She blocked a yawn. 'What time is Fergal getting here?'

'Early, he hoped, when I called him.' Liam slowed and turned the Land Rover into the driveway. Switching off the engine, his eyes gleamed down at Nikki. 'He's pretty excited, too.'

'Well, he would be.' Nikki gave a mysterious half-smile. 'He planted the idea in the first place.'

CHAPTER TWELVE

CHRISTMAS EVE.

'Just grab my arm and beam,' Liam instructed as they stepped into the party atmosphere.

'Oh, my goodness!' Nikki clung tightly. 'Can this be our little community hall?' Eyes wide in disbelief, she looked around her at the tables set so beautifully, so bold with colour, as if the people had decided to thumb their collective noses at the dreariness engendered by the drought and welcome in Christmas with a bang.

Amazingly, from somewhere the decorating committee had found a richly checked fabric of red, green and blue for the tablecloths. Blue sparkling wineglasses were juxtaposed with the red of the Christmas crackers and the green and white of the serviettes.

And the Christmas pine, right from the magnificent star at the top down to the simple clusters of popcorn gathered in gold net and hung with bright red ribbon, was a sight to behold.

'Are you sure we haven't stumbled into Aladdin's cave by mistake?' Liam shook his head in wonderment. 'It's stunning.'

Nikki swallowed the lump in her throat. 'It certainly is…'

'But not nearly as stunning as you,' he declared

softly. Dipping his head, he kissed her gently but thoroughly for all the world to see. 'You take my breath away.'

'And you take mine, Doctor.' Nikki gave a shaky laugh, her heart cartwheeling, and she wondered whether it was possible to overdose on sheer happiness.

'Well, aren't you two a sight for sore eyes?' Grace bore down on them. 'Nikki, you look divine.'

'Thank you, Grace,' Nikki fluttered a hand to the aquamarine silk of her slim-line dress. 'You look lovely, too.'

'It's so exciting!' Grace almost did a little jig, her face wreathed in smiles. 'Just everyone's here. We've been waiting for you—but not long,' she qualified. 'Did you have an emergency?'

Liam's eyes gleamed wickedly. 'Not quite.'

She lent forward confidentially. 'Do you know, the weather bureau's predicting rain and I fancy I saw some rather promising cloud formations earlier. Wouldn't a huge summer storm be a perfect end to the evening?'

Liam and Nikki merely exchanged a lingering smile.

'Nikki, you look gorgeous!' Dressed in a Christmassy-looking skirt and slinky top, Jade made her way between the tables towards them. 'My stars!' Her voice ran up a note. 'Is that a Von Traska model you're wearing?'

Nikki beamed. 'I had it flown out especially for this evening.'

'Hey, don't I get a mention, too?' Liam pretended to puff out his chest. 'I did shave, after all.'

Jade giggled. 'You look gorgeous, too. Black shirts on dark-haired men look very sexy. Now…' She referred to her clipboard. 'You're both up here on the official table. Follow me.'

'Jade…' Nikki looked at Liam helplessly. 'Why are we at the official table?'

Jade flapped a hand. 'Because you were the driving force behind all this—especially you, Nikki. And because Fergal said so.'

Nikki's dress dipped gracefully around her ankles as she reluctantly followed Jade. 'This was a community effort,' she tried to reason. 'It wasn't just me!'

'Rats,' Jade dismissed, waving them gracefully to their chairs. 'You were the wind beneath everyone's wings—with apologies to whoever wrote those words.' She chuckled.

When everyone was settled, Fergal rose and called for hush. 'This is a very special evening,' he said, his gaze moving warmly around the gathering. 'And I want to congratulate each and every one of you for your planning and hard work and for giving of yourselves so generously to make this a Christmas to remember.'

A muted 'Hear, hear,' echoed around the hall.

Fergal beamed. 'Now, before we partake of this wonderful feast, there is one other very special announcement. Earlier this evening I was privileged to be celebrant at the remarriage of Wirilda's medical officers, Liam Donovan and Nikki Barrett.'

Someone shrieked and then wild clapping broke out. 'You sly dog, Liam!' came from Baz Inall's table.

'How perfectly lovely,' Grace sighed, and began dabbing her eyes. 'And I never guessed.'

'What about a toast, then?' someone urged. 'Dion? You're good at making speeches.'

'Just keep it short,' a wag called from the rear of the hall.

Dion rose to her feet obligingly, congratulating the newly-weds, adding with a touch of dry humour, 'You may or may not know, Liam insisted on donating this marvellous champagne. I'm wondering now whether he had a secret motive all along.'

That statement brought a ripple of laughter, before Dion continued, 'Liam and Nikki have given unstintingly of themselves for this community and I know I speak on behalf of us all when I wish them every happiness for the future. So, if we could all be upstanding, and raise a toast to Liam and Nikki—the Doctors Donovan.'

'Oh, help.' Overflowing with emotion, Nikki held tightly to Liam's hand. 'Did you know this was going to happen?' she asked.

Liam's smile began slowly, then widened. 'I had a fair idea Fergal was up to something.' A brief frown touched his eyes. 'Did you mind it was such a small wedding?'

She shook her head. 'It was perfect. *This* is perfect.' She drew her hand in an arc around the faces in the hall.

'Ah, look like dinner's being served.' Liam made

an elaborate show of massaging his stomach. 'I could eat a horse.'

'Horse isn't on the menu as far as I know.' Nikki sipped her champagne in an attempt to bury her giggle. 'Are we going to have dancing later?'

'Bound to. Someone mentioned a band.'

Much later, over coffee and dainty mince pies, Nikki asked, 'Do you think Grace's clouds will come to anything?'

Liam chuckled. 'She's hardly ever wrong.' He leaned across and refilled their glasses. 'And Cubby Daylight said he'd *smelt* rain for days now.'

'Is that possible?'

'Oh, yes,' Liam said seriously. 'Our indigenous folk have uncanny perception about things like that.'

'How come we get to have our own bottle of champagne?' Nikki looked at him through a haze of happiness. 'Is it because we're the bride and groom?'

'Probably.' Liam's smile was tender. 'Are you a tiny bit drunk, Mrs Donovan?'

She giggled, as she was meant to. 'Drunk on happiness. I love you, Liam.'

'I love you, too—so very much.' He picked up his glass. 'Shall we have another toast? A private one?'

Her mouth twitched. 'I think we should have several.'

'OK, you first.'

Nikki pretended to think. 'What about to the best Christmas of our lives and to all our wonderful patients who are mostly our friends as well?'

'I'll drink to that. But may I add another very special one?'

'Go on, then.' She smiled indulgently, running the tip of one finger lightly down his shirt front.

'To my wife, Nicola,' he said, his voice deep and husky with emotion. 'And to this, our new beginning.'

Modern Romance™
...seduction and
passion guaranteed

Tender Romance™
...love affairs that
last a lifetime

Medical Romance™
...medical drama
on the pulse

Historical Romance™
...rich, vivid and
passionate

Sensual Romance™
...sassy, sexy and
seductive

Blaze Romance™
...the temperature's
rising

27 new titles every month.

Live the emotion

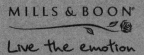

Medical Romance™

OUTBACK MARRIAGE by Meredith Webber

It was bad enough that Blythe Jones had to sit next to rude, challenging – and dangerously attractive – Cal Whitworth at a wedding. It was definitely too much when his plane crashed and the two doctors had to spend a night in the wild. And as for his plea for Blythe to work in his Outback practice...well! Blythe was finding it harder and harder to remember she was off men!

THE BUSH DOCTOR'S CHALLENGE
by Carol Marinelli

Dr Abby Hampton is the ultimate city doctor, and is dreading being stuck in a bush hospital for three months. But when she steps off the plane, midwife Kell Bevan is there to greet her – and he's absolutely gorgeous! The sexual chemistry between the two is ignited – but Abby is determined not to get involved.

THE PREGNANT SURGEON by Jennifer Taylor

High-flying surgeon Joanna Martin has learned not to risk her heart for any man – including her new senior registrar Dylan Archer, even though her secret desire for him is strong. But Dylan's determination to break through his boss's cool exterior finally results in one night of passion – and then Joanna discovers she's pregnant...

On sale 2nd January 2004

Available at most branches of WHSmith, Tesco, Martins, Borders, Eason, Sainsbury's and all good paperback bookshops.

1203/03₄

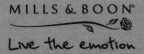

MILLS & BOON®

Live the emotion

Medical Romance™

THE REGISTRAR'S WEDDING WISH *by Lucy Clark*

Annie Beresford is a talented surgeon and trainee consultant – but her wish is for marriage and children before it's too late. She knows that falling for her new boss, Hayden Robinson, is a bad idea – but he might just be the one. She knows they can't be happy without each other – even if he won't believe her...yet!

THE DOCTOR'S RESCUE *by Kate Hardy*

When GP Will Cooper rescues a toddler from a busy road and ends up in hospital himself – with a broken arm and leg – he also discovers a beautiful stranger, Dr Mallory Ryman, by his bed! And then Will asks her to be his locum – and live in his house to care for him while he recovers!

THE GP'S SECRET *by Abigail Gordon*

GP Davina Richards is content with her life, caring for the Pennine community she grew up with – until her sexy new boss arrives! Dr Rowan Westlake has eyes only for Davina, but he has a secret, and she's not going to like it. His only hope is that facing the past will allow them to face the future – together!

On sale 2nd January 2004

Available at most branches of WHSmith, Tesco, Martins, Borders, Eason, Sainsbury's and all good paperback bookshops.

1203/03b

The *Midnight* Hour

Celebrate the New Year...
with a gorgeous new man!

Kate Walker   Kate Hoffmann   Lilian Darcy

On sale 2nd January 2004

*Available at most branches of WHSmith, Tesco, Martins, Borders,
Eason, Sainsbury's and all good paperback bookshops.*

FREE
4 BOOKS
AND A SURPRISE GIFT!

We would like to take this opportunity to thank you for reading this Mills & Boon® book by offering you the chance to take FOUR more specially selected titles from the Medical Romance™ series absolutely FREE! We're also making this offer to introduce you to the benefits of the Reader Service™—

★ FREE home delivery   ★ FREE gifts and competitions
★ FREE monthly Newsletter   ★ Exclusive Reader Service discount
★ Books available before they're in the shops

Accepting these FREE books and gift places you under no obligation to buy; you may cancel at any time, even after receiving your free shipment. Simply complete your details below and return the entire page to the address below. *You don't even need a stamp!*

YES! Please send me 4 free Medical Romance books and a surprise gift. I understand that unless you hear from me, I will receive 6 superb new titles every month for just £2.60 each, postage and packing free. I am under no obligation to purchase any books and may cancel my subscription at any time. The free books and gift will be mine to keep in any case.

M3ZED

Ms/Mrs/Miss/Mr ....Initials ....
BLOCK CAPITALS PLEASE

Surname ....

Address ....

....

....Postcode ....

Send this whole page to:
UK: FREEPOST CN81, Croydon, CR9 3WZ
EIRE: PO Box 4546, Kilcock, County Kildare (stamp required)

Offer valid in UK and Eire only and not available to current Reader Service subscribers to this series. We reserve the right to refuse an application and applicants must be aged 18 years or over. Only one application per household. Terms and prices subject to change without notice. Offer expires 31st March 2004. As a result of this application, you may receive offers from Harlequin Mills & Boon and other carefully selected companies. If you would prefer not to share in this opportunity please write to The Data Manager at the address above.

Mills & Boon® is a registered trademark owned by Harlequin Mills & Boon Limited.
Medical Romance™ is being used as a trademark.